THE REVOLUTION OF
Sabine

THE REVOLUTION OF

Sabine

BETH LEVINE AIN

CANDLEWICK PRESS
CAMBRIDGE, MASSACHUSETTS

First edition 2008

Library of Congress Cataloging-in-Publication Data

Ain, Beth Levine.
The revolution of Sabine / by Beth Levine Ain. —1st ed.
p.   cm.
Summary: During Benjamin Franklin's visit to Paris in 1776, sixteen-year-old Sabine Durand rails against the strict rules of society and her social-climbing mother by rejecting her arranged marriage and spending more time with servants and others who accept Franklin's political ideals and those she read in Voltaire's *Candide* while having her portrait painted by the renowned artist Fragonard.
ISBN 978-0-7636-3396-7
[1. Social classes—Fiction. 2. Mothers and daughters—Fiction.
3. Conduct of life—Fiction. 4. Self-actualization (Psychology)—Fiction.
5. Arranged marriage—Fiction. 6. Franklin, Benjamin, 1706–1790—
Fiction. 7. Fragonard, Jean-Honoré, 1732–1806—Fiction.
8. France—History—Louis XVI, 1774–1793—Fiction.]   I. Title.
PZ7.A277Poi 2008
[Fic]—dc22   2007022121

2 4 6 8 10 9 7 5 3 1

Printed in the United States of America

This book was typeset in Scala.

Candlewick Press
2067 Massachusetts Avenue
Cambridge, Massachusetts 02140

visit us at www.candlewick.com

For Jon

Chapter One

Sabine closed her bedroom door softly behind her. She walked, holding her breath, down the hallway and paused at the top of the staircase. Downstairs, the house was buzzing. Sabine could hear Cook shouting frantic commands at his staff and the maids shuffling around on hands and knees, polishing the floors one last time. The flowers had arrived, and everyone was surely waiting with frayed nerves for Mother to come and either approve or dismiss them.

Sabine began her descent, stepping all the way to the left side of step number twelve to avoid its creaky spot. If she could just get out for a little while, she could make it through the rest of the day. She needed air. *Three more steps and I'll be down the stairs and through the front door,* she thought as she stared at her feet. *One . . . two . . .*

"Sabine!" Madame Margaux Durand was standing with her arms crossed at the bottom of the staircase. She had appeared out of nowhere.

"Mother," Sabine said carefully. "I was just on my way down to—"

"Honestly, darling, let's not start the lies this early in the morning. This is far too important a day for your usual nonsense. All of Paris has been vying for an invitation to our home to meet Mr. Franklin, and you're trying to sneak away. Do you have any idea how important this is for me, for our family? Do you know how many girls your age envy your position?" Without giving Sabine a chance to answer, her mother continued: "Now, turn yourself around, go have a bath, and wait for Brigitte to come help you get ready for the party." Madame Durand uncrossed her arms and shooed her daughter away, back up the stairs, back into the long hallway that led to Sabine's suite, back into the room that, despite its grandeur, felt like a prison cell to Sabine. She was trapped.

Sabine threw herself onto her bed, and the giant satin duvet fluffed up all around her. She wished she could sink right into the mattress and disappear. All that would be left when Brigitte came to find her would be the small indentation of a sixteen-year-old girl. A girl, it would come to be known, whose mother had driven her to insanity and who, on the morning of the biggest ball to be thrown in Paris in an age, had simply vanished.

"Sabine." Her governess poked at her cheek impatiently. Sabine blinked and looked up; she had fallen asleep in the bathtub. "You could have drowned!"

"Wouldn't *that* have ruined Mother's ball?" Sabine replied wearily as she hoisted herself out of the tub and into the towel Brigitte held for her. "Actually, no," she said, rethinking. "I'm sure she wouldn't have let that happen. She simply would have told the guests that I had come down with a cold or something, and then she'd smile, sip her champagne, and plan to deal with the details tomorrow."

Brigitte played along with Sabine. "You're probably right. Only I'm sure she wouldn't have had the time to handle the details first thing in the morning. She'd have too much gossip to tend to. Who was wearing what, who had had too much to drink—"

"Who hadn't paid enough attention to her!" added Sabine. "She'd have wanted to wait until afternoon, at least, to call for the coroner." Sabine laughed, and Brigitte, who was shaking her head, followed her into the dressing room. "Now, let's get me into this gown, shall we?" Sabine asked.

There was a knock at the door, and Brigitte went to answer it. From the dressing room, Sabine heard Brigitte's voice rise up, and she peeked around the corner out of curiosity. She recognized the profile of Brigitte's son, Michel, whose face hadn't changed since he was a little boy. Fair-skinned with deep, dark eyes and black hair, he was handsome, if a bit scruffy. Though she and Michel had been friendly as children—back when Sabine was a little rougher around the edges than her mother would have liked—their young friendship had come to an end long ago. Sabine had no use for him now. But he was Brigitte's son, so the Durands all tolerated his presence in the household from time to time. It was the reason he was even allowed upstairs. He had special consideration. Michel and his mother were very close, and Sabine had to admit that Michel was a good son for coming by so often to see his mother— even if it meant Sabine had to tolerate him when she wasn't in the mood.

Madame Durand hired Brigitte Bernard when Sabine was just a baby. She had come highly recommended, but she had a small baby herself, and she would have to care for him in addition to Sabine. This was permissible to Madame Durand only because Brigitte had been the governess to a highly regarded family and that was just the kind of governess she had been seeking—not because she wanted Sabine to have the best care, Sabine knew. But because she wanted everyone in Paris to know that her daughter had the very best governess.

Michel had been a wonderful built-in playmate for Sabine, and he had always helped around the house, particularly with the gardening—he had a natural green thumb. But as they grew older and became teenagers, Madame Durand felt that it was time for him to go find work somewhere else. Brigitte had threatened to leave if Margaux wouldn't hire Michel to her staff—she would not have been able to bear being away from her only son. So Madame Durand had a choice to make: lose her daughter's governess, who was by that time a favorite and trusted employee, or take on Brigitte's illegitimate son as a member of her staff. It really wasn't a difficult choice at all, but Margaux made it a dramatic one, and both Brigitte and Sabine had fretted for days while she kept them in the dark. Sabine was in a panic over the possibility of losing her governess. When Margaux finally did decide, she did not tell Sabine herself. Brigitte did.

Madame Durand had done something rather reasonable, actually. She had asked Dr. Chaumont's family if they could use Michel's help on their staff. The Chaumonts weren't aristocrats, so it wouldn't be the kind of environment Michel had grown used to, but it was better than nothing. The Chaumonts happily took Michel on as gardener. Sabine always suspected that they didn't need a gardener at all but that they thought it was the right thing to do. They didn't live very far from the Durands, so Brigitte could see her son as often as she pleased. It was a solution that satisfied everyone. Most of all, Sabine was thrilled. Brigitte meant the world to her, and the thought of losing her had shaken Sabine more than she let anyone know.

Sabine pulled back into the dressing room

abruptly now. She would be utterly embarrassed if Michel happened to get a look at her, and besides that, Brigitte would have her head.

When Brigitte returned, she was muttering something about Michel's delinquent friends.

"What was that all about?" Sabine asked casually. She hadn't seen Michel in quite a while and wondered what brought him into their home today of all days.

"Nothing you have to worry about, Sabine. Michel is just being Michel. He wants to drive me to an early grave is all."

"Is he still running with Dr. Chaumont's son and his friends? Étienne, right? Such a silly bunch of boys, really. I can't believe Michel would even like them." The truth was that Sabine had always been rather interested in the Chaumonts, even before Michel went to work for them. Though they weren't part of the Durand circle, they were a much respected family about town, given the doctor's impeccable reputation. No one would have anyone else care for them. When she had a cold or was ailing in some way, Sabine was always happy to visit the doctor's office, which was on the Chaumonts' property. She begged her mother to go to his office rather than have him come to them. It was a rare opportunity to go somewhere else, somewhere different. For some reason Margaux indulged it. There was something about Dr. and Madame Chaumont that she found charming. They had an easy manner about them. They didn't seem at all invested in the goings-on in various Parisian social circles.

The Chaumonts were what Mother called bourgeois. This was essentially a word for the upper middle class, a class Margaux was intensely afraid of. Although she and her husband, Georges, were technically aristocrats, Georges' family money had dwindled substantially over the years—due in large part to Margaux's extravagant, social-climbing ways— and they were barely in the same league as most of those in their class. This clearly haunted Madame Durand. The thought of people working for money in the way Dr. Chaumont did seemed to threaten her very existence. And yet even she had to admit that the Chaumonts were good people. The doctor was an excellent one, and Madame Chaumont was lovely, if a bit undignified and less kempt than she should be. Sabine shared her mother's view—but did not like Étienne. She had found him cocky in their few encounters and wondered how a person in a lesser position would feel comfortable acting this way with someone such as herself.

Sabine was also surprised that Étienne and Michel had become good friends. It wasn't usual for members of any higher class to fraternize with those in the peasant or wage-earning classes. But she gathered from Brigitte that the Chaumonts had become like a second family to Michel. Since he didn't have a father, Brigitte was grateful, and yet she still felt that it wasn't quite proper and that maybe Michel was something of a cause for the Chaumonts. She had told Sabine that she hoped they wouldn't change their minds one day and leave this overeducated peasant boy to his own devices once again. Brigitte always worried about Michel. He was everything to her.

"He doesn't just *like* them," Brigitte said. "He believes all their talk about revolution and the end of the monarchy. God forbid. Can you imagine? He spends all of his extra time either at the Chaumonts' dinner table or at that tavern, discussing books. Books! I should never have let Dr. Chaumont convince me that Michel should read. Why should he need to read? He should mind his own place and respect the way things are. You know," she continued, having a thought, "I remember when the two of you were little, romping around the garden together, pretending you were king and queen. Maybe all that pretending put him in the mind that he wasn't just a governess's son." Brigitte looked wistful and worried. "Well, let's forget all that. Tonight, you must be the belle of the ball!"

Carefully, Brigitte helped Sabine into her gown— layer upon layer of crinoline and golden satin on top of what was surely one of the tightest corsets in Paris—Madame's orders. Then she worked on Sabine's hair and added a hint of rouge to her face and some powder to the tip of her nose. "*Voilà!*" Brigitte exclaimed when she had finished.

"Well, let's have a look at me," Sabine said eagerly. "We mustn't keep Mother waiting, after all. She might go searching for a replacement." She got up and walked toward the mirror that leaned heavily against the wall. She looked at herself and sighed. She knew her face so well—the deep brown eyes, rosy lips, and plump cheeks, the dark hair that always fell loose no matter how much Brigitte twisted it into shape. And the small shoulders that bore the weight of the biggest ball gowns in town with ease. She was accustomed to how she looked in the mirror, but more and more lately, she felt sad when she looked at herself for too long. Sabine felt that at the end of the day, the way she looked was meaningless. What did any of this matter?

"You're lovely, Sabine." Sabine knew that Brigitte had noted the solemn look on her face and was trying to change the mood. "Will Élodie be at the ball?"

"Élodie? Miss a chance to meet the one and only Mr. Benjamin Franklin—the brilliant American, the man who tamed lightning? He's about all the women of Paris could dream of, and Élodie *does* consider herself a woman of Paris! I believe she's only one notch less preoccupied with this party than Mother."

Mr. Franklin had only just arrived in France, but Madame Durand hadn't missed a beat. She wanted to be the first one in Paris to have him in her home. Though she had always planned on throwing her annual winter ball, she quickly changed course and let everyone know that this year's ball would be in the American's honor.

"And Élodie plans to arrive fashionably late, so she can make a special entrance," Sabine added. "Of course, her parents wouldn't allow anything else. Why can't Mother and Father be more like the Fourniers? Everything about them is effortless. Madame Fournier makes Mother look like a peasant girl, all dressed up in last year's fashions for a party that happened two days ago." Sabine felt Brigitte studying her as she grimaced.

"Don't frown, Sabine. Your face might stay that way." Brigitte was always saying silly things like this. Sabine adjusted her expression, though. *Just in case she's right,* she thought with a smile. The truth was Sabine wasn't really jealous that Élodie's mother was more elegant than her own. She was jealous that Élodie had a mother at all, a mother who was more concerned with her daughter's well-being than her own place in Paris society. Brigitte continued, "And Sabine, you mustn't talk that way about your mother. She just wants everything to be perfect for tonight. This is very important to her. It should be exciting for you, too. Mr. Benjamin Franklin in this house! I think I'd better freshen up myself! Let's go down now."

Sabine appreciated her governess's excitement—she was a little excited, too, she had to admit—and gave her a quick hug. "Brigitte, I was thinking about what you said before about Michel. When he and I used to play in the garden, I don't think we ever pretended to be king and queen."

"What, then?"

"We were pretending to be American colonists, setting sail for the New World, building houses, foraging for food, things like that. It was rather silly, I suppose. But what I mean to say is, I don't think the king and queen ever interested him at all."

Chapter Two

When Sabine made her way down the stairs this time, her mother was nowhere to be found. Brigitte was busy managing the train of Sabine's dress as she glided toward the grand hall, where the ball was set to take place.

On her way, she passed by the sitting room and spotted, out of the corner of her eye, a portrait of Benjamin Franklin hanging above the fireplace. When Margaux had heard that Mr. Franklin was on his way to Paris, she had become fixated on acquiring a portrait of the man. There was something about this Franklin that was making the women of Paris society swoon, and Sabine thought it all rather silly. He didn't look particularly handsome to her, and besides, he was one of the American colonists who had betrayed the king of England. Why would anyone of any status find such a man charming? But Sabine was glad for her mother's sake that the portrait had arrived in time for the ball.

The sun was on the verge of setting when she opened the door to the empty room and the light through the leaded glass windows turned everything to gold. Sabine dismissed Brigitte to go let her mother know that she was downstairs and ready to be seen, and then she walked to the window. She floated past the long tables set to perfection with crisp linens, silver, crystal, and grand flower arrangements that looked as though they might have been plucked from the pastel garden in a painting that hung in her father's study—Sabine's favorite. The room was exquisite, and in a few moments it would be ruined—lip rouge staining the crystal, the smell of perfume overwhelming the fresh flowers, and gossip polluting the perfect acoustics.

Sabine unlatched the window and breathed in the cold December air. She had been seeking this relief all day. *How is it that a house this grand can feel so stuffy?* she wondered.

"Oh, Sabine, *chérie,* you are the portrait of loveliness."

Sabine pulled herself inside in a flash, nearly hitting her head on the window. Élodie stood before her.

Élodie Fournier had become Sabine's best friend soon after Sabine and Michel had stopped playing together. Madame Durand had been delighted to finally find her daughter an appropriate playmate; she immediately seized the opportunity to turn her boyish daughter into a lady and set up lunches and tea dates with other society girls. Sabine was downright bored at every lunch but one. Devilish even as a young girl, Élodie had instantly made Sabine laugh, so they became fast friends.

Once, when they'd grown closer, Élodie said to Sabine, "We were all wondering when you'd grow out of that dreadful governess's son. Thank goodness it didn't last any longer. You might have ruined your reputation for the long haul!" Sabine had cringed at the mention of Michel. She was embarrassed that someone like Élodie had known that her best friend until that moment had been a servant. Just the same, she'd laughed at her new friend's comment to show that she had indeed grown out of Michel, all the while wondering if it might have been Michel who had grown out of her.

"Élodie!" Sabine said now. "What are you doing here? I didn't hear you come in. What happened to your grand entrance?"

Sabine studied her friend and smiled. No matter how well put together Sabine felt before she saw Élodie, she felt positively disheveled as soon as she stood before her friend. Élodie's dress was extraordinary, of course, but it was the way she carried herself that was so striking. From her straight back and relaxed shoulders to her gliding walk and the signature feather in her hair, she was confident and at ease in a way that made Sabine feel ten years old.

"Never mind that," Élodie replied with a wave of her hand. "I was too excited and had Claude bring me over early to be with you. Why do you have the window open?" she asked.

"Just getting some air. This house had been absolute madness for days, and Mother hasn't let me out." Sabine knew she could tell Élodie anything, but she would never be able to make her understand why opening a window and breathing in deeply calmed her so. She wasn't even sure she understood it herself.

"Well, you'd better close it before your mother catches you," Élodie replied.

As if on cue, Madame Durand appeared at the doorway. "Sabine, close the window this instant. If a wind blows in, it could ruin everything." Sabine and Élodie exchanged a knowing look.

"I'll take care of it, madame." Élodie gently

brushed Sabine aside and pulled the window shut. "There," she said as she turned back toward Sabine and her mother. "Now, what else must be done to keep things in order, madame? Let us help."

Sabine stood still as her mother took Élodie by the hand and showed her around the room. She could hear Margaux raving about Élodie's dress as they walked away from her. Usually Sabine was hurt when her mother displayed more interest in her friend than in her, but at this moment, she was just the slightest bit annoyed at *Élodie*. Sometimes, it felt as if Élodie sought attention from Margaux. But Sabine dismissed the thought almost as soon as it occurred to her. Élodie was charming and well mannered—that was all. Sabine was just relieved that Margaux hadn't said anything negative about the way *she* looked.

Soon the sky turned indigo and the first couple was walking through the Durands' front doors. The entrance hall started to fill up with all the smells and noises Sabine had anticipated. Powdered noses and wigs left trails of dusty romance behind as they mingled together. Sabine had always found that the routine of everyday life in the upper crust of Parisian society was offset only by events such as these, and she relished them. Tonight was no exception.

The gowns were beautiful—the women still followed the trends of King Louis XV's mistress, Madame de Pompadour, whose style had set the fashion for all the high-society women in France. Though the king had changed mistresses, the women of Paris had not. More than ten years after her death, they continued to layer themselves in taffeta with deep necklines leading to chest plates made of bows. The gowns dripped elegance, with tufts of lace softening their elbows and appliquéd silk flowers hemming every flounce. And the men were equally striking in their brocade knee-length jackets, their knickers and tights, with cravats of lace at their necks and big ribbons tying back their hair. They were almost as pretty as the women. All the rooms of the house glittered and hummed. Sabine's mother was right, of course. All girls her age *would* give anything to be at this ball. They'd give anything to be part of her family, of her world.

Sabine thought about this for a moment. It excited her to think of who she was and what she had, and she wouldn't trade any of it—not her education, not her wardrobe, and definitely not her status. And though *sometimes* when she looked in that mirror, she felt as if she were pretending to be something she wasn't, she realized, looking around the room tonight, that she mustn't be the only one. In fact, with all the wigs, powder, and false smiles whirling around the room, the ball might as well have been a masquerade party.

When Madame Durand had determined that the right people had arrived, the doors to the grand salon finally opened. It was important to Sabine's mother that the sighs of admiration came from the highest up in society, so she positioned them not so subtly at the very helm of the crowd for the opening. And sigh they did. The room was exquisite, the music pitch-perfect. The pavane, the traditional processional dance, played, and in danced all the beautiful couples, taking long, gliding steps, the ladies' hands resting on the back of the men's. As the ladies swept their dresses up off the floor and strutted like peacocks on the arms of their partners, Sabine wondered about her own future. *Whom will I enter the ballroom with one day? Will I love him? Will I be happy then?* Sabine felt young to be thinking of such things, but the truth was, she had been somewhat consumed with it lately due to Élodie's interest in marriage. Her friend did seem ready to take on society on her own and maybe even run a household. She seemed so much older and more settled than Sabine.

Élodie found her way to her friend after the crowd moved in. "Did you see Madame de Colbert?" Élodie whispered with her fan perched on the tip of her nose. "Why, her bosom practically fell out of her dress when she curtsied!" She giggled, raising one eyebrow. Élodie was always lethal.

"At least she is a married woman, dressing that way." Sabine was suddenly in the mood to gossip herself. "Her daughter, Sophie, is pouring out of her dress, too! Honestly, how will she ever find a respectable husband if she carries herself so improperly?"

"She won't, but in that family, *respectable* probably isn't at the top of their list. I should think they'd just want to marry Sophie off to the first man who asks—a cad with lots of money, no doubt—which would explain why they are showcasing her that way. It ought to be as easy as attracting bees to honey!" The girls giggled into their fans until Sabine's mother shot them a look from across the room and they were forced to straighten themselves up.

Élodie fanned herself and scanned the room. "Where *is* that Mr. Franklin?"

Sabine was wondering the same thing. "Mother must be going mad. The ball's success rides on his shoulders, after all. If he doesn't show up, I do believe she might faint from shame."

"But if Mr. Franklin does show up, I think half the women in this room will faint. And I will be proud to be among them!" Élodie made a dramatic gesture, slapping her hand to her chest as if she were the heroine of an opera.

"Well, there are many other wonderful people here tonight. Monsieur Fragonard is in attendance—did you know?" Sabine spied the famous painter over the top of her fan and nodded in his direction. He was pale, and peering over his glass of champagne, his deep-set eyes seemed rather tired but intense. The lines on his face and his balding head aged him, making him look more the part of a politician than an artist. Again, Sabine wondered what all the fuss was over Mr. Franklin. She'd take an artist over a politician any day.

"Fragonard, the artist? I would love to be painted by him. Wouldn't it be divine to sit for a portrait?" Élodie asked dreamily.

"I don't think so at all. I think it would be a bore," Sabine replied. "Well, not a bore so much as a waste of the artist's time. The king's mistress or a baron's daughter—they would make a wonderful portrait, but Sabine Durand? I don't think so!" she exclaimed, thinking of all the paintings hanging in their house and all the stories she told herself about the people in them. She loved to get lost in art.

"You forget, Sabine, that your father is a prince." Sabine understood that Élodie was being kind. Georges Durand was a prince in title only. He had little influence and no ambition, and this drove Margaux mad. If it were up to Georges Durand, the family would barely register on the society scene at all. He had even dropped his title from their society surname. Without it, *Durand* sounded positively bourgeois. And to Margaux, status meant everything. She did not marry a prince only to fall into obscurity. For her, every day was spent trying to advance her reputation and become a force in Parisian society. And even though Sabine enjoyed the benefits of her mother's ambition, she thought Margaux seemed desperate and it embarrassed her.

"Yes, of course he is," Sabine replied. "But much as I would like to, I don't fancy myself a princess!"

"Well, you should, Sabine. We're as close as anyone to being princesses!" Élodie smiled coyly at Sabine as the music for a quadrille started to play and they spotted the de Croy brothers, Jean-Philippe and Paul, approaching. *My mother's doing, no doubt,* Sabine thought with a sigh. Margaux had been trying for months to make a match for Sabine with Jean-Philippe. He and his twin brother were the most eligible young men in town—they were the sons of the *duc* de Croy—and Sabine would be a fool not to be flattered by Jean-Philippe's interest in her. Besides, it could be worse. He was fair-haired and strapping; his blue eyes sparkled, and his smile gleamed. Sabine had to admit he was awfully handsome.

"Ladies, we would be honored," Jean-Philippe

said as the two young men tipped their heads down and held their hands out.

Élodie and Sabine knew their place. On cue, they curtsied and held out their hands. Suddenly, the magic of the ball was in full force. The music roared, and Jean-Philippe whisked Sabine around the room in dramatic fashion. She felt graceful and outside of herself. The whole room was a watery painting to her now, the people and the colors turning to streaks as she whirled through the candlelit hall. She could hardly see faces, just barely she glimpsed her mother nodding approvingly, her father shaking hands with the *duc* de Croy, and Brigitte peeking in from the drawing room. But then Sabine blinked to be sure that what she saw next was real. Monsieur Fragonard—painter to aristocrats, *artiste extraordinaire*—was studying her from his table.

The music ended, and Sabine and Élodie curtsied again to their dance partners. The four of them stayed close for the rest of the night, pretending to have much to say to one another. They all played their parts well—the boys doting on the girls, the girls obliging with coy, ladylike interest. Sabine found this a difficult role to play; she wasn't sure she liked Jean-Philippe. He seemed utterly without elegance to her. If he was so wellborn, so well educated, and such a catch, why did she notice him staring at Sophie de Colbert every time she came into view?

But Sabine knew that for Élodie this was no act. As composed as her best friend was most of the time, she fell apart inside when Paul de Croy was in sight.

The night passed quickly, and each time the ballroom doors opened, the crowd would turn their heads, hoping that Mr. Franklin had arrived. But the night came and went without Mr. Franklin's presence, and Margaux Durand was devastated. To her guests, she tossed it off as bad American manners. "How will they manage to run a whole country when their leaders behave this way?" she had said to

Madame Fournier as she laughed a nervous laugh that only highlighted her embarrassment. And later, when the last carriage carried the last guest away, she walked solemnly up the stairs without a word to Sabine or Georges. Father and daughter stood there in silence.

At least with her mother, Sabine had a way of communicating. It was insincere and often angry, but they still spoke to each other. With her father, it was always like this: the two of them left alone in the wake of Margaux with nothing to say. Georges simply touched his daughter's sleeve and stuttered out a "Good night, darling" before he ran after his wife.

Sabine stood alone in the entrance hall as the house suddenly fell quiet and still. She was sad that it was all over, and in spite of herself, she was sad for her mother, too. Sabine knew this night had been a complete failure for her mother. She found herself wishing that the ball had been everything Margaux had wanted it to be. She was suddenly aware of how desperately she wanted her mother to be happy. And as she headed back up the staircase that she had descended so many hours ago, avoiding the creaky step out of habit, Sabine wondered if Margaux would ever wish the same for her.

Chapter Three

The breakfast hour brought with it just the kind of furor Brigitte and Sabine had imagined the day before. The scent of buttery pastries hung over the heads of a staff busy trying to make the house look as if the ball had never happened. Already, calligraphied notes had begun arriving, thanking the Durands for a lovely evening, all of them having the good manners not to mention the absence of Mr. Benjamin Franklin. But the most important note had come from Mr. Franklin himself, apologizing for his failure to appear. He had come down with a terrible cold and was unable to leave his residence in Passy.

Madame Durand was visibly relieved by this news and made arrangements to have Cook send some fresh baked goods out to Mr. Franklin's residence in the country right away. She also made sure to respond to every single note she received with a carefully placed mention of Mr. Franklin's apology. *Thank you so much for coming. What a shame that Mr. Franklin's bad health kept him from joining us. He sent his apologies this morning.* Margaux Durand simply wouldn't have people going through their day feeling sorry for the woman whose party was stood up by the American.

Sabine came down to join her mother in the midst of all the letter writing and was greeted with surprising news.

"Ah, Sabine. You must get dressed right away. Monsieur Fragonard has agreed to paint your portrait, and he is expecting you this afternoon." Margaux said this without looking at her daughter, who stood just a few feet from her.

"Good morning to you, too, Mother," Sabine replied deliberately. Madame Durand put down her quill and shot her daughter a look. Sabine quickly retreated. "Why would he want to paint me?" she wondered.

"*He* doesn't want to paint you, darling. *Your father and I* want him to paint you. When I saw him watching you dance with Jean-Philippe last night, I thought he seemed interested enough in you for me to commission a painting. He painted for King Louis the Fifteenth, you know. It is an honor that he even agreed to do it." Before Sabine could object, her mother continued. "Incidentally, I have to write a note to Jean-Philippe today, thanking him for escorting you around the dance floor. It takes an awfully graceful young man to make you look light on your feet. And don't worry, I'll be sure to apologize for your clumsiness."

"Mother"—Sabine tried to ignore the insult—
"I'm not sure what to wear for the portrait. I imagine
Monsieur Fragonard has more important things to
do or more important people to paint than me. Perhaps we should cancel."

"It isn't a matter of importance, Sabine; it is a
matter of financing. He'll paint you because, like all
good patrons of the arts, we're paying him to. Don't
worry yourself about it. I've had Brigitte lay out a
dress for you, and the carriage will take you to his
studio. Have something to eat and go." With that,
Margaux turned back to her note writing, and Sabine
knew that the discussion was over. She was deflated.
Up until that moment, she had believed that artists
painted people who interested them. She hadn't realized that all those portraits were probably commis-
sioned by wealthy people. In an instant, her mother
had robbed Sabine of her love of art. The romance
was gone. She took a piece of crusty bread, slopped
some jam on it, left the dining room, and headed to
the kitchen. She preferred to eat out of her mother's

sight so there would be no criticism of her manners or her figure. In the kitchen, Cook was preparing Mr. Franklin's croissants and Brigitte was sitting at a table with her coffee.

"Come and sit, Sabine. Have your breakfast with me, and tell me all about your dance with Jean-Philippe de Croy!" Brigitte was cheerful as always.

"It was nothing, Brigitte. He is nothing but a good dancer with a wandering eye."

"I doubt that, Sabine. I'm sure he has eyes only for you." Brigitte's optimism on this subject annoyed Sabine. Most times she thought Brigitte was on her side, but then she'd blindly go along with Margaux on something like Jean-Philippe, and it made Sabine doubt her governess's loyalty.

"And what prince are we speaking of this morning? Could it be the one and only Jean-Philippe de Croy? Or is it Paul? Is there even a difference?" Michel had come up behind Sabine as she was talking, startling her. *Why on earth is he here?*

"This is none of your business, Michel," Brigitte

replied. "But, if you must know, it was Jean-Philippe, who just happens to come from one of the best families in Paris, and the only girl he asked to dance all night was our Sabine."

"Is that right?" Michel asked, raising his eyebrows. "Well, then, when's the wedding?" Sabine knew Michel was being sarcastic, and she rolled her eyes. Just then, Brigitte was called to the dining room by Madame Durand, and Cook went out to the pantry. All at once, Sabine and Michel were alone, and Sabine didn't know what to say.

"I hardly think we'll be planning a wedding anytime soon, and anyway, what do you care?" She was trying to be cool with Michel. Even though she really couldn't imagine marrying anyone, let alone Jean-Philippe, for some reason she wanted Michel to think she wouldn't quite mind if she did marry one of the de Croy brothers someday.

"You're right. I don't care. I was making conversation," Michel said with similar coolness. "So, what kind of big plans do you have for the day, Sabine?

You and Élodie have important things to discuss, no doubt." He said this as he picked up the bread and jam she had left on the table and shoved it into his mouth.

Sabine was seething at the way he brushed her off. "For your information, I'm off to have my portrait painted by the artist Jean-Honoré Fragonard." She was suddenly very proud of this fact.

"Finally," Michel whispered in her ear as he got up to leave the kitchen, "the princess sits for her portrait."

Sabine wasn't sure what Michel was talking about, so she changed the subject. "Michel," she said, stopping him as he headed out the door, "your mother is worried about you spending so much time with Étienne Chaumont. Why do you insist on hanging around that group? You work for him. You're not bound to him."

"I don't work for Étienne; I work for his parents, and he and I have some very important things in common. It only bothers Mother because she's afraid that if I think too much, I might turn into something other than a governess's son." He looked at Sabine seriously for a minute, as if he were willing her to react.

"What could Étienne Chaumont possibly have you thinking about besides wine? And what's wrong with being a governess's son, anyway?" This was the most Sabine had spoken to Michel in a long time, and she was feeling a little out of her element.

"Perhaps you should come along with me sometime and see just what kind of thinking we do, and maybe then you'd understand that being a governess's son isn't so bad. It's that I don't get any choice in the matter. Just as you don't have any choices, Sabine." Michel was staring at her now, and she felt exposed. She was relieved when Brigitte came back in and hurried her upstairs to change.

In her dressing room, Sabine's thoughts drifted back in time as Brigitte hooked Sabine into the gown Margaux had chosen for her.

"Sabine! Come look at this one." Michel was in the library staring at a painting of a lovely girl sitting on a blanket by a river, surrounded by people frolicking in the grass. Sabine knew it well—it was one of her favorites.

Sabine caught up to Michel and stared up at the painting. She and Michel were all of ten years old; both were damp with perspiration from running around the garden all morning, now pausing to catch their breath while they examined Georges Durand's art collection. "I bet she's a princess," Sabine said, panting. "I bet she's a princess whom everyone sits around and admires all day long."

"Admires for what?" Michel asked, still staring at the painting, his mouth hanging open and his cheeks flushed from the spring air outside.

"Well, for being a beautiful princess, of course." Sabine turned to look at Michel now.

"Why should she be admired for that? If she's a princess, then she didn't have a thing to do with it." Michel was always challenging Sabine, and it annoyed her.

"Many people admire my father because he is a prince, you know."

"They don't admire him, Sabine. They have to be nice to him because he is a prince—that's all. Doctors and artists ought to be admired more than princes, and besides, your father isn't a real prince. He just comes from a long, long, line of princes and is lucky enough to get to keep the title."

"A prince is a prince, Michel. And a governess's son is just that. Don't go forgetting that now." With that, Sabine stormed out of the room.

Now, as she stood in her dressing room, holding on to a bedpost as Brigitte pulled her corset tight, she winced at the memory of her friendship with Michel. How had she forgotten? After that day, the tension between them had only gotten worse. Michel had become increasingly confrontational with her, and she had begun to resent him. Before that, she had adored him—adored running around with him, pretending to be whatever wonderful characters he imagined for them, and studying all of her father's paintings together. And then, just as their friendship began to deteriorate on its own, Margaux decided she'd had enough of it herself. She placed restrictions on Michel—he was to fraternize only with the children of the staff and never, ever with Sabine. The decision gave Sabine and Michel just the excuse they needed to end their childhood friendship once and for all.

At first, it had been hard for Sabine. She would still wander outside to the pantry where she and Michel used to meet in the afternoons after Sabine's lessons. She would hope that he would ignore her mother's orders and still want to be her friend. After all, neither one of them had ever been known to obey the rules. But after a few days of showing up to find no one there but Cook, grumbling about a missing spice or a bunch of rotten potatoes, Sabine had finally given up. It was time, she had decided, to move on. And once he left to work for the Chaumonts, the ties were cut for good. For years now, she and Michel had rarely spoken to each other. And as on the previous day, when Michel had come to speak with Brigitte, it was usually Sabine who avoided Michel. She was curious, though, why he had suddenly paid a visit to his mother two days in a row.

The carriage ride to Monsieur Fragonard's studio took Sabine and Brigitte on a winding tour of Paris. Although Sabine was anxious about having her portrait painted, she was grateful for the ride. The air was crisp and the trees barren, and Sabine thought about how much she preferred autumn to winter. She thought of the few jewel-toned leaves that had covered the trees just a month ago. Those leaves reminded her of the ladies' dresses of the previous evening. Too fast, the leaves had turned brown and brittle, the trees shedding them quickly, just as the ladies, when they had gotten home last night, set aside their dresses, looking forward to next season's colors.

Sabine also enjoyed the bumpiness of a carriage ride. Gliding around a marble dance floor was all right last night, but today and most days she preferred cobblestones. She liked to feel the ground beneath her just as she liked to suck in the outside air. Besides, her mother was right. She was *not* graceful on the dance floor. It took a masterful dancer to make her feel as she had during her dance with Jean-Philippe. On the cobblestones, though, Sabine was sturdy and sure of herself. She never tripped, never wobbled, and took a man's hand as she got out of the carriage only to be cordial. What kind of a lady was more comfortable navigating the old stone streets of Paris than she was the smooth floor of a ballroom?

When they arrived at the studio, Antoine, the driver, opened the door for them, and they approached the little door of a town house. Sabine and Brigitte had to climb a flight of stairs up to the second floor, where the artist worked. They entered a room that smelled of oil paints and damp stone, and Sabine's shoulders relaxed. She was pleased to be in such a space. After a moment, the artist came in through a side door and greeted them coolly.

"*Mademoiselle Durand, oui?*" He barely looked at Sabine.

"*Oui, monsieur.*" She curtsied as she spoke. "Thank you for agreeing to paint me. I have seen your work, and I must say it is an honor for me . . ." She trailed off as he walked away from her, gathering materials, setting up.

"Why don't you sit over there, and we'll get started?" Fragonard motioned to the corner of the room, where a stool was set up by a railing. Sabine walked over and sat on it, trying to keep her back straight. Brigitte, meanwhile, took a seat near the door.

"Are we doing a profile, then?" Sabine asked this nervously. She never thought she was very pretty from the side.

"Yes, but you're slouching, mademoiselle. Can

you sit up a bit straighter?" He wasn't rude exactly, Sabine thought, but he wasn't kind either.

Sabine tried to do as he told her, but the extra-tight corset Brigitte had tied her into seemed to be failing her. Plus her stomach had started making noises, which reminded her that Michel had eaten her breakfast. Sabine hoped the artist hadn't heard. She rested her left arm on the railing for support and laid her other hand in her lap, but she felt awkward.

"This won't do." Fragonard put down his brush and went in search of something. When he reappeared, he was carrying a pillow. It was a giant, faded plum-colored velvet pillow, and he placed it directly behind Sabine's back, against the wall. It cushioned her perfectly, and she was relieved. The artist went back to work, and Sabine tapped the fingers on her right hand restlessly against her lap.

"Could you hold still, mademoiselle?"

"*Pardon, monsieur,*" Sabine answered in a whisper. Just then, her stomach acted up again letting out a slow hunger groan. From across the room, she heard Brigitte stifle a laugh. Sabine chuckled, too. Brigitte's giggle, even when she tried to stifle it, was contagious. The artist put down his brush again and left the room, giving Sabine a moment to compose herself. This time, though, he returned with a book. He handed the dusty little volume to Sabine, and she looked at him curiously.

"Have a look at this, mademoiselle. Perhaps it will distract you for a little while." He then went on to place the book, which was open to the first page, in her restless right hand. Sabine was embarrassed that she had to be treated like a child, but calmer now that she had something to hold on to. She glanced down and began to read.

There lived in Westphalia, at the country seat of Baron Thunder-ten-tronckh, a young lad blessed by nature with the most agreeable manners. You could read his character in his face. He combined sound judgment with unaffected simplicity; and that, I suppose, was why he was called Candide.

How lovely, Sabine thought as she flipped the book cover closed and looked at the title. *Candide,* by Voltaire. She had heard of Voltaire but didn't know he had written a novel, and she absolutely loved to read novels.

Sabine flipped back to the first page and read on. Inside, she found Candide in an embrace with Cunégonde, the baron's daughter. Theirs was a forbidden love because Candide was the illegitimate nephew of the baron. Breathless, Sabine read about how Candide was sent away when the love affair was discovered. And how when Candide heard that Cunégonde had been murdered, he didn't believe she was dead and carried on loving her, hopefully.

The story had Sabine positively entranced, but every once in a while, in spite of herself, she remembered that she was being painted. And though her mother had stolen some of her faith that art captured the most interesting of people, Sabine did hope— she really did—that her portrait, despite its subject, would be special to look at.

As she listened to Fragonard work across from her, she self-consciously pictured her own portrait. The saffron color of her dress, saturated but soft against the pillow the artist had found, which was the exact same shade of plum as the bow in her hair, the bow that Margaux had chosen to match the bow at the bosom of Sabine's dress.

As the hour went by, the hand that had been resting on the railing dropped as Sabine became more engrossed in the book. *Does he mind?* Sabine thought. *Should I move it back?* But she was familiar with Fragonard's work, or rather she had overheard someone at the ball describing it. He was one to focus on the fine details of his subject. In the case of Sabine it might be the highlights in her hair, the blush in her cheeks, the changing shapes and shadows of her dress as she breathed, and her fingers, her restless fingers, which had finally found peace wrapped around the book. The studio was quiet as he painted. The only noises came from

Sabine's belly and from Brigitte, whose deep wheezing as she nodded off in the corner filled the room with its rises and falls.

"You'll need to come back once more, mademoiselle." Fragonard's voice startled Sabine out of Candide's imaginary world. She blinked a few times. *Come back? To the studio?*

"I was sure it would take only one sitting," Sabine said in a slightly spoiled voice. Sometimes, she did act like a princess.

"I usually do need only one session, but the light is changing. Will you come back the day after tomorrow at the same time? We should be able to finish up quickly then." The artist paused and then continued. "I'll keep the book for you. It made a nice pose." This compliment made Sabine blush, and it also reminded her that the book was not hers. *Yes*, she thought, *I would love to come back the day after tomorrow and read more of* Candide!

"Oh, I suppose so," Sabine said to Monsieur

Fragonard as Brigitte draped her cloak around her shoulders. Sabine gathered her skirt to walk back down the stairs. "See you then." No need for him to think she was happy about it.

Chapter Four

The ride home proved to be rather more of an adventure than the ride to the studio. The sky had changed from clear and deep blue to dark gray and wet. Sabine and Brigitte had just made it into the carriage when the heavens opened up. The horses did their very best to navigate through the downpour, but the streets filled so quickly that their driver couldn't see the potholes anymore. Suddenly, the carriage lurched forward, throwing Sabine against Brigitte, who was sitting facing her. Then the carriage stopped completely. One of the horses had gotten its leg stuck in a muddy hole. They were going nowhere.

"Antoine!" Brigitte shouted to the front. "Won't you run to the house and send a new horse for us?"

"Nonsense," Sabine replied. "We can certainly make it from here. We're only a few steps from home." She started to unlatch the door when Brigitte swatted her hand away.

"Don't be ridiculous, Sabine. Your mother would have my head if you came in covered in rain and mud. And imagine if someone spotted us trudging through the rain. They would think we were street people."

"Oh, Brigitte. Who cares, anyway? I'm not waiting here for another carriage. Father is playing cards today at the Fourniers, so there is no other horse to send. Come; I'm going." This time, she opened the door so fast that Brigitte had no choice but to follow her.

"Mademoiselle!" Antoine had popped open an umbrella over their heads. "Please, slow down and let me lead." He was clearly desperate not to let anything happen to Sabine, as no servant wanted a confrontation with Madame Durand. However, Antoine was trying so hard to keep the ladies covered that he fell right into a hole in the road filled with muddy water. He tried desperately to get up, but kept slipping. Sabine put out her hand to help him up, but he refused.

"Antoine, take my hand!" Sabine demanded. Brigitte was holding the umbrella over Sabine's head as Antoine finally took the girl's hand. But even Sabine—graceful on the cobblestones, sturdy on unsteady surfaces—couldn't stand firm on the slippery ground and instead of helping him from the mud puddle, went flying into it herself.

As she and Antoine sat there, covered in mud, the cold rain pouring down on them, Brigitte simply stood by, howling with laughter. Sabine would have none of this. She held out her hand to Brigitte for assistance, and Brigitte, who finally composed herself, obliged. Sabine took the hand gratefully but

decided at the last moment to include her dear governess in the fun and pulled her down into the mud
with them! Brigitte was horrified, but Sabine was
delighted. She was an absolute mess, but she didn't
care. The damp, cold air against her face turned
her cheeks red, and she felt excited to be alive. And
there they sat—the driver, the governess, and the
princess—laughing, kicking, and splashing as the
rain came down all around them.

If it hadn't been for Michel, they might have sat
there all day. But just a few moments into their
mishap, he came upon them. He was walking in the
direction of the Durand home once again. He almost
passed them by, but on second look, must have realized who these soaking wet, mad people were and
stopped to admire them. Laughing, he helped them
each to their feet. When Sabine took his hand, she
was suddenly ten again and Michel was pulling her
out of a pile of leaves in the garden. She had gotten
butterflies in her belly then. How had she forgotten

that? Sabine composed herself. She had been a silly little girl once—that was all.

"Thank you, Michel," she said, and even offered a quick curtsy, as if that might correct the image of her splashing around in the mud with his mother and Antoine.

"Yes, Michel," Brigitte said, still laughing, "thank goodness you found us!" She coughed then. At first it seemed like she was trying to clear a tickle from laughing so hard, but soon the cough was so loud and raspy that they all stopped and looked at her with concern. Michel went to her immediately and put his arm around her to help her settle down. "I'm fine, Michel," she said between coughs. "I just laughed a bit too hard!"

"I'm sorry, Brigitte," Sabine said. "I should have listened to you and stayed in the carriage."

"No, no!" Brigitte insisted. "You were right. Adventure does a person good every once in a while. And, well, laughing feels pretty good, too." Noting the concern still lingering on the faces of Michel and Sabine, she said, "I'm fine! Who ever got sick from laughing too hard?" Then she gathered herself and started walking.

The rain died down to a mist as they all trudged slowly away from the scene of their accident. Antoine was silent and embarrassed and walked ahead of them toward the house, probably hoping that this whole incident would be over soon.

"What possessed you to think you could walk home in that downpour?" Michel asked the group, but he was looking intently at his mother.

"Oh, it's my fault," Sabine said. "I think Candide's adventure put me in the mood for some adventure myself!"

"*You're* reading Voltaire?" Michel was visibly shocked.

"Yes, I am." Sabine hadn't realized that this would be interesting to Michel, and she began to feel rather proud of herself. "Why not? You're not the only one who can read, you know."

"Well . . . do you like it?" Michel seemed very interested in Sabine now.

"I've just started it. It seems like a good enough read." Sabine was trying to act as though she read books like this all the time. For some reason, she wanted to impress Michel.

"Well, if you get stuck on something, or if there is anything you might want to discuss, I've read the book myself, and I'd be happy to help you along," Michel offered quietly.

"*You've* read *Candide*?" Sabine said with a smirk. "That's quite all right, really," she said coolly. "I think I should be able to manage a simple book without help from . . ." She paused. She was about to say "someone like you," but she measured her words. "Without any help at all," she said.

Michel shrugged her off and turned his attention back to his mother. "I was on my way to bring you that tea we discussed this morning, Mother."

Brigitte seemed to brush him aside as she grabbed the little brown bag he handed her. In the meantime, they had arrived at the Durand house. Still muddy and wet and shivering from the winter air, the four of them made quite an entrance as they tumbled into the foyer through the front doors. Sabine had thought her mother would be upstairs, dressing for dinner, but instead, there she sat, tea-cup in hand, next to Élodie, whose eyebrows almost reached her hairline in surprise.

Why would Élodie be here now? Sabine thought. Surely her mother wouldn't have invited her for tea knowing that Sabine had an appointment.

"What on earth happened to you?" Madame Durand's voice was stern. She stood up at once and walked toward the damp group.

"*Madame, s'il vous plaît.*" Antoine started to explain what had happened to the horse, but Sabine inter-rupted him.

"It was nothing really, Mother. One of the horses got stuck, and I insisted that we walk the rest of the way home. Brigitte and Antoine had no choice but to follow me. Unfortunately, we met the same fate as the horse and fell into some mud ourselves. But then Michel happened by and helped us out of our mess. It's all fine now, really. Let's all go clean ourselves up." Sabine noted that Élodie seemed to be sizing her up, and she wondered why she sometimes felt that she couldn't trust her dearest friend.

"Go on, then," Madame Durand commanded, as if it had been her idea. "Sabine, go fix yourself up and come join Élodie and me for tea. We were just having the most wonderful chat about the de Croy brothers. It seems they'd like to see the two of you again." She turned her attention to Brigitte and the driver then. "Brigitte, you go on along, too. Antoine, you'd better go dig that horse out of the mud and have the carriage cleaned before Monsieur Durand returns home." She looked away from the group with a sigh and returned to Élodie.

"I'll be just a moment, Élodie," Sabine remarked to her friend with a broad smile. "Oh, and Mother, I should think you'd want to thank Michel for helping us as he did."

Michel had already turned to walk out toward the front door when Sabine said this. He stopped and turned back toward her now. Sabine was surprised at herself. *Why did I insist on this?*

"Yes, of course. Thank you, Michel" was all Madame Durand could utter.

Michel, never taking his eyes off Sabine's, replied in kind: "It was my pleasure."

When Sabine came back downstairs, she found Élodie sipping her tea alone. She shook off her paranoia about Élodie being there. Margaux must have thought Sabine would be home in time. In fact, she might have, if not for their mishap in the rain.

"Élodie, darling! Where did Mother go off to?" Sabine kissed her friend and picked up a teacup. Just then, Cécile, the maidservant, rushed in to pour the tea.

"Thank you, Cécile," Sabine said warmly. She was Sabine's favorite servant besides Brigitte, whom she didn't really think of as a servant. Cécile was young and sweet, and Sabine suspected that she was carrying on an affair with Antoine. Sabine suddenly felt a pang of envy. Cécile's life seemed so much more romantic than her own.

"Your mother went to lie down. I think you've exhausted her with your antics," Élodie responded.

Sabine noted that Élodie, like Margaux, always thought of Sabine as someone who engaged in antics, and this irritated her now. She got up and went to the window. She opened it and leaned outside. She was in search of that same feeling the damp air on her skin had given her earlier. She leaned out the window even farther, and when she turned to the left, toward the pantry, she saw Michel leaning against the building, staring in the other direction. She studied him—aware that Élodie was chatting about something behind her. Michel's dark hair was unkempt, and he seemed a bit dirty. But the longer strands of hair rested perfectly on the cheekbones and jaw that had turned his boyish face into a man's. His shoulders were still rather frail, though.

At sixteen, his body still had to grow into his face. Sabine had never really looked at Michel so closely. She realized now that there might have been a good reason for this—there was something about him that made it hard to look away.

"So, Sabine," Élodie continued, "Michel certainly seems to be back in your good graces. I do wish you'd be careful. Your mother is intent on making a match between you and Jean-Philippe. I'm sure he wouldn't like to hear of you carrying on with the help." Élodie paused, then cried out, "Sabine!"

Sabine pulled herself back inside and turned to Élodie.

"What on earth is so interesting outside?" Élodie asked impatiently. "Your cheeks are positively crimson. Did you even hear what I said?"

"Yes, of course I heard you," Sabine said. She could tell that Élodie was suspicious of her mood, and again, her friend's distrust annoyed her. She thought Élodie was actually hoping that her suspicions came to something just so she could be right.

This was one of the traits Sabine could have done without in Élodie, but she forgave her friend because they had grown so close over the years. They had grown out of girlhood and into young womanhood together. Sabine couldn't imagine doing that alone.

"Michel simply helped us out of the mud, Élodie—that's all. And since when do you care what Jean-Philippe likes and what he doesn't? Didn't you see him eyeing Sophie de Colbert all night at the ball? I thought we decided that any young man who was interested in her would surely be a cad." Sabine assumed that her mother had put Élodie up to this, and, for the third time in under an hour, she felt annoyance at her friend, this time for having complied with such a request.

"Oh, never mind that," said Élodie. "Men cannot be expected to be saints, after all. I only care about you, Sabine. Imagine how wonderful life would be if we each marry one of the de Croy twins. Why, we would be sisters! And you would finally be free of your mother."

"Free of my mother and bound to Jean-Philippe. That would just be an exchange of one prison for another, I imagine. No, thank you," Sabine replied.

"The de Croy brothers are handsome and rich. Not such a terrible prison, I think." Élodie was defensive. "Unless you were thinking of running off with Michel to live the glamorous life of a peasant? Yes, I could see how tempting that might be."

"What is this, Élodie? All this suspicion because the governess's son helped me out of a mud puddle this afternoon?" Sabine was quick to scold her friend. "Besides, you and I are already sisters. Even if you marry Paul de Croy and I marry someone else, we will be sisters still. And anyway, I would like to decide for myself whom I will marry. Now, you haven't even asked me about having my portrait painted! Ask me now, and let's forget about Michel and Jean-Philippe for a while."

Élodie smiled at her friend, but Sabine could tell that she was irritated with her. "Yes, do tell me all about your sitting," Élodie said.

Sabine went on and on about the studio and the artist, and she even mentioned the book she had picked up, which was clearly of no consequence to Élodie. Her friend nodded at her as she spoke, but to Sabine it seemed that she was doing so out of politeness only and was busy thinking about something else entirely.

When Sabine had finished gushing, Élodie clapped her hands together and said, "Marvelous, Sabine. I cannot wait to see the finished painting. Now, you must join my parents and me at the opera Saturday night. You'll come and sit in our box, all right? Wear something gorgeous! We'll pick you up at seven o'clock."

As usual, Sabine didn't actually get to think about whether or not she'd like to go. With Élodie, everything was "must." She made demands, and Sabine went along. In this way, Élodie was very much like Margaux. In fact, she was like Sabine's mother in a great many ways, and Sabine often wondered why she found it so easy to be friends with Élodie yet so difficult to live with her mother. Nevertheless, Sabine was thrilled at this chance to go to the opera. The opera, like a big ball, was magic to Sabine, like one of her stories about the paintings in the house come to life. "Yes, of course, Élodie. I look forward to it."

With that, Élodie was out of her seat. "Divine. Now, get some rest, and Sabine?" she said, turning back.

"Yes?" Sabine asked.

"I don't blame you for having a little thing for Michel—any girl could see the appeal. But listen to me: do leave it alone. He's the help, darling. Nothing but the help."

Sabine smiled a small smile at her friend as she left but felt for some reason as if someone had knocked the wind out of her.

Chapter Five

Jean-Philippe was due to arrive any minute. They were to take tea together, and Sabine's mother was downstairs, in a tizzy over the arrangements. If she knew that Sabine was immersed in thought and not grooming herself for this event, Margaux might just explode.

But as Sabine was dressing, she grew lazy and wistful and wanted only to lie on her bed and think about Candide and Cunégonde and art and love.

"Oh, Sabine, not again." Brigitte was standing over her now, and Sabine knew she was in trouble. She had been like this since the day before, doing nothing but staring at her bedroom ceiling. "Jean-Philippe will be here any moment, and you are not ready to receive him. Your mother will have both our heads if you are not downstairs and impeccable in the next ten minutes!"

Sabine found it rather comical when Brigitte tried to be firm with her. She sat up and hopped off the bed to humor her governess. "I'm ready, Brigitte. I was just taking a break for a minute."

"I don't know how it is that a book could have you so preoccupied, Sabine," Brigitte said with a cough. She knew what Sabine had been daydreaming about because it was the only thing she had talked about since yesterday.

"I honestly don't know, but I've seen you with your book of poems, Brigitte. Don't you feel the same way about it?" Sabine noted, knowing full well that Brigitte couldn't read. But Sabine had seen that book of poems and wondered about it.

"Well, yes, that was a gift from Michel. He reads them to me sometimes, but I don't even know what the poems mean. I just like the way they sound. Now, you need lip rouge and powder, and your hair is falling out of its knot because you were lying against the headboard. Honestly!" Brigitte was exasperated and started coughing heavily.

"Brigitte, calm down. Everything is going to be just fine. Besides, isn't it better manners for me to make an entrance? I wouldn't want to be sitting there waiting for Jean-Philippe, twiddling my thumbs. I should arrive in my own time just when he's had a moment to wonder what might be keeping me. Really, you and Mother are much too eager. It isn't very ladylike." Sabine turned away from Brigitte, knowing that she had shocked her governess with her calm. She was smiling inside at the game she was playing. The truth was, Sabine had no interest in Jean-Philippe whatsoever. And it is easy to gamble with something you don't care very much about.

They heard voices traveling up the staircase from the foyer now, and Sabine knew she couldn't hide any longer. She nodded at Brigitte, and the two of them headed downstairs.

There was Jean-Philippe, very formally dressed and looking positively stuffy. His face was chiseled and bright, but he looked cold to Sabine, like someone who never noticed the help unless they did something wrong—much like her mother, in fact. Besides, he was vain. Mirrors fascinated him.

"*Bonjour, Monsieur de Croy.*" Sabine curtsied deep at the knees and held out her hand. Her caller took her hand and brushed it with his dry lips.

"*Bonjour, mademoiselle,*" Jean-Philippe replied as Sabine stood up straight. "You are a vision as always. But please, call me Jean-Philippe. So kind of your mother to invite me for tea." With that, he nodded toward Madame Durand and then winked at her. Sabine found this difficult to bear. Her mother, on the other hand, was clearly enamored.

"Please, monsieur, won't you escort us to the parlor? Oh, and Brigitte, do go and see how the tea is coming along." Madame Durand had put on the voice she reserved for company. It was so cloying, Sabine made a mental note not to add any sugar to her tea. She would like it bitter today.

Madame Durand sat down with Sabine on the sofa, and Jean-Philippe sat across from them in an armchair. They chatted idly about the ball, the food, the music, the guest list. Jean-Philippe complimented Madame Durand's impeccable taste and called her one of the last true aristocrats. Margaux was pleased as punch. Sabine sat silent until the conversation turned to the weather and how it had calmed down after yesterday's sudden storm. Finally, she had something to add.

"Yes, the storm was quite something. We had a bit of a mishap in the carriage and—" In the middle of her laugh, her mother cut her short.

"Yes, the carriage was stuck for a moment on Sabine's way home from Monsieur Fragonard's studio. He is working on her portrait."

Sabine was furious that her mother had interrupted her, and tried again. "The carriage was stuck and I insisted on walking the rest of the way, but then the driver fell in the mud. Well, I tried to help him out of course, but in I went, too. And then Brigitte! Can you imagine the spectacle?" Sabine talked fast and loud so that her mother wouldn't attempt to quiet her.

Laughing, Jean-Philippe said, "Well, aren't you an independent young woman, traipsing through the mud so valiantly? Wherever did you come by such bravado? From you, madame?" He said this while smiling at Margaux, who feigned amusement at Sabine's antics, but Sabine could tell that her mother was not pleased. Nevertheless, Sabine liked that Jean-Philippe was interested in her story and hadn't made her feel silly for telling it. Jean-Philippe continued, "So, do tell me. How did you all get out of this mess?" He looked intently at Sabine now.

"Well, luckily—" Sabine was interrupted right away this time.

"Sabine, let's talk to Monsieur de Croy about something more interesting. Surely he's heard enough of this little trial. Jean-Philippe, have you had the pleasure of meeting Mr. Franklin since he's been in town?"

"Yes, of course, madame. *Dr.* Franklin is quite a man." He was correcting Margaux. "I understand why all the women of Paris are so wrapped up in him. I see you have his portrait above the mantelpiece— they are all the rage these days, eh?" He gestured to the painting and then made sure to add, "And what a shame that he couldn't attend the ball. I heard of his illness. But perhaps you will join us for supper with him at our house."

"Why, that would be divine, wouldn't it, Sabine? Another occasion for the two of you to spend time together, and for us to make the acquaintance of *Dr.* Franklin." Margaux nodded as she said this. She seemed proud of herself for noting Jean-Philippe's correction. Sabine had heard Franklin referred to as both *Mister* and *Doctor.* She was certain that it didn't matter at all and that Jean-Philippe was patronizing her.

"Jean-Philippe . . ." Sabine had thought of something she'd like to discuss. She had heard her father refer to Franklin as a revolutionary as if this were a good thing, and she wasn't sure she saw it that way at all. "You seem awfully knowledgeable about Mr. Franklin." She made sure to emphasize *Mister*. "Don't you think it's peculiar that we in Paris are so enamored of this Benjamin Franklin when he is leading the colonists in a revolt against their king? We are so very loyal to our king. We wouldn't be so pleased, I imagine, if someone came along and incited this kind of revolution here, would we?"

Jean-Philippe rolled his eyes and sighed dramatically. "And this is why politics are better left in the hands of men, Sabine. It would be too complicated for me to try to explain over tea. Perhaps we can resume this conversation another time."

"Yes, Sabine. Let's be ladies and leave such matters to the politicians," Margaux said dismissively. "And speaking of tea, where *is* that Cécile?" Margaux was looking very nervous as she excused herself to go scold the staff, leaving Sabine and Jean-Philippe alone. Jean-Philippe took this opportunity to sit by Sabine on the sofa.

Immediately, Sabine sensed a change in the mood. Perhaps he had sat down just a little too close. Surely, this was a mistake on his part. Sabine inched away a bit, but Jean-Philippe only inched closer.

"You know, Sabine, I've heard about your feisty side." Jean-Philippe said this as he placed one hand lightly on her knee and leaned in toward her. "That is partly why I've remained so interested in you despite your family's questionable status."

Sabine tried again to inch away from him. "My family's *questionable* status seemed all right with you moments ago when you were complimenting my mother."

"Sabine, you and I both know that your family wants nothing more than a marriage into the de Croy family. And it is entirely possible. You're pretty enough, and frankly, you're more interesting than my other options, so let's let down our guard a bit, no?"

"Monsieur, what my mother wants and what I want are two very different things. Now, would you mind removing your hand from my knee?" Sabine shifted her body away from him, but Jean-Philippe took her arm firmly and looked fiercely into her eyes. Just then, the door swung open and Cécile stood before them with a tray of tea in hand. Sabine was so relieved.

"Not now," Jean-Philippe said sternly in Cécile's direction, and for a moment Sabine thought Cécile would listen to him. Cécile looked at Sabine and at the firm grasp Jean-Philippe had on her wrist. Sabine gave her a look that she prayed Cécile would recognize as panic. And Cécile, God bless her, seemed to understand instantly what was going on.

"Oh, monsieur, forgive me. The kettle . . ." She fumbled for words in a way she never did, and

Sabine knew she was stalling. But Jean-Philippe interrupted her.

"I said, not now," he growled, this time waving his hand in dismissal.

"*Pardon, monsieur,*" Cécile said again, and started to back up through the door, when she dropped the entire tray full of hot water and china.

"Oh, Cécile, please don't worry about it. Here," Sabine said, her voice a little shaky, "let me help." She took the opportunity to loosen her wrist from Jean-Philippe's grasp. He looked at her with anger in his eyes and finally saw fit to release her. Sabine practically ran to Cécile. She picked up spoons and teacups and very slowly tried to scoop sugar off the floor with her hands. She was desperate not to be alone with Jean-Philippe and relieved to have a task to distract her until the moment passed.

Jean-Philippe just stood there for a few moments, watching the two women try to clean up, until he finally broke the silence. "Is this your maidservant,

Sabine? I must say, it's awfully kind of you to help, darling, but really. The sight of you on your hands and knees isn't exactly appealing."

Sabine stopped what she was doing and looked at the floor. Her face was burning. She felt humiliated and embarrassed and wasn't sure what to do next.

Cécile looked at her mistress, then at Jean-Philippe and said, "The way you're talking, monsieur, I would think you'd rather like sight of her on her hands and knees."

Jean-Philippe clenched his jaw. "Get a handle on your help, Sabine," he fumed. "No woman in my circle would ever let their servants talk that way."

"I think you've well established that I'm not quite worthy of your circle, Monsieur," Sabine said, suddenly emboldened by Cécile.

"That will be all now, Cécile," Jean-Philippe said in a once and for all way. He was still looking at Sabine, though—staring at her with anger and perhaps admiration. She wasn't sure. He wouldn't look at Cécile. It was as if she were so beneath him that he couldn't bear to lay eyes on her for too long. Sabine felt guilty for even knowing someone who behaved this way.

Just then, Madame Durand came back through the door from the kitchen with Brigitte in tow. She was visibly upset at the sight of the sugar all over the floor.

"Cécile!" She was almost shouting. "What have you done? And Sabine, get up off that floor! You are entertaining a guest." She looked at Brigitte. "Brigitte, I think you'd better have a chat this evening with Sabine about her manners." Then she looked at both Cécile and Brigitte and said, "That will be all for both you. Cécile, hurry along and make some more tea, and be careful this time, for goodness' sake. And, Brigitte, well, we'll talk later."

Both Brigitte and Cécile made to leave, with Brigitte begging everyone's forgiveness on behalf of Sabine. Sabine made a note to herself to explain to Brigitte what Cécile had done for her. She hated that her mother had humiliated them just after Cécile had been such a help. Sabine made sure to give an extra nod to Cécile when she looked at her, silently thanking her for her bravery. Once they were both gone, though, she felt nervous again and wanted this visit to be over.

"Mother, I'm suddenly feeling rather ill. I think I might be sick. Won't you entertain Jean-Philippe? I think I must retire. I'm terribly sorry, monsieur," she said in one breath as she gave a brief curtsy and backed out of the room.

In her bedroom, Sabine caught her breath. She could still feel Jean-Philippe's hand wrapped around her arm, and it made tears spring to her eyes. She pulled her reading chair over to the window, which she then pried open an inch. She sat there for maybe an hour or more before she was interrupted by a seething Margaux Durand.

Sabine's mother barged in the room, shouting. "Just what on earth did you think you were accomplishing down there? This was your chance to make an impression. For *some* reason, this young man is interested in you, and you behave like a girl who is expecting proposals from every man in town!"

"Mother, would you please let me explain? I don't think you'd be very pleased with him if you knew how he treated me when you left the room. You know, if it weren't for Cécile—"

"Sabine, honestly, between Michel and now Cécile, I'm beginning to think we're right back where we started. I thought I took care of it years ago—your special affection for the lowest class. All this time, you and Michel have all but ignored each other, but now he's rescuing you from the mud and Cécile, *Cécile*"—she repeated her name, clearly to emphasize her disbelief—"of all people, is disrupting a perfectly lovely afternoon with Jean-Philippe. Well, I won't have it."

"Mother," Sabine began, rising from her chair as anger rose inside her, "Jean-Philippe put his hand on my knee and sat so close, I couldn't breathe. When I pulled away, he even grabbed my arm. It was only because Cécile walked in the room that Jean-Philippe let go. *Now* aren't you grateful toward her?" Sabine was sure her mother would be reasonable after hearing the truth. She didn't want to have to tell her what Jean-Philippe had said about Margaux.

"Sabine." Her mother took a calmer tone. "Jean-Philippe is a young man who is very interested in getting to know you. I'm sure you misinterpreted his behavior. Frankly, you haven't spent much time with refined young men, and perhaps you were confused by his flirtation. Now I must write him a note apologizing for your behavior. I'll tell him you'd be delighted to see him again once you're feeling better." She paused for a moment and then spoke again: "I think I'll also mention that, as he suggested, we should join his family for supper along with Mr. Franklin whenever the *duchesse* de Croy would like to host us."

Sabine nodded knowingly at her mother's calculations. Once again, this was all about Margaux's interests. Why was Sabine so committed to protecting her mother from the things that Jean-Philippe had said when her mother wasn't at all interested in protecting *her*?

"Yes, Mother. You do that," Sabine said.

"Good." Margaux turned and started for the door. "Now, get some rest, and we'll see you at supper."

Chapter Six

Sabine was on her way to Fragonard's studio—without Brigitte this time, because she was tired and needed a rest. Sabine had tried to explain to her governess what Cécile had done for her the other day, but Brigitte just muttered something about it being none of Cécile's affair and how she had no business speaking to Monsieur de Croy that way. Sabine was only a little surprised by this reaction. The truth was, Brigitte was as set in her ways as Sabine's mother—she, too, believed that rules were the most important thing in the world. It struck Sabine after her conversation with Brigitte that both Margaux and Brigitte were afraid to live without rules. This way, they knew where they belonged.

Sabine was actually feeling a bit guilty about Brigitte—her governess had spent much of the previous two days washing out the dress Sabine had wrecked in the mud on the way home from the first portrait sitting, and it had been quite a task. Somehow, though, Brigitte had managed to get it in beautiful shape once again, and Sabine was so grateful, it was she who had suggested that she go to the second sitting alone. Her mother wasn't around to object, and that was that. Antoine would have to act as her chaperone. Certainly he would rather sit in the studio than outside in the cold with the carriage, anyway.

Sabine was happy to be riding by herself for once and was looking forward to sitting for her portrait again. In fact, it was knowing that she was going back for her second sitting that had gotten her through a painful supper with her parents the night before. Her mother had insisted on gushing about Jean-Philippe to Monsieur Durand, who seemed indifferent to the whole matter. This annoyed Sabine. She would almost like her father much more, she had thought, if he were as insistent as her mother about such things. But instead he acted as if Margaux were discussing someone else's daughter. "Yes, that's nice, darling. . . . I'm sure he's a fine young man, indeed. Good man, the *duc* de Croy. Yes, yes, yes."

And it was really no wonder, Sabine had thought. The way Margaux went on and on about such inane details, like the buckles on Jean-Philippe's shoes. "Oh, I'm just sure they were made by the king's shoemaker. The de Croys are very close with the king, you know. . . ." Sabine was in desperate need of a distraction from her life—the life her mother had invented for her—and she couldn't wait to get back to *Candide*.

This time, when she arrived at the top of the stairs to Fragonard's studio, she found the artist sitting at his easel, studying his work. He gave a start when she cleared her throat to announce herself. Fragonard quickly covered the canvas with a cloth.

"*Pardon, mademoiselle,*" he said. "I would rather you not see the work until it is final."

"Of course, monsieur," Sabine said as she curtsied. She was secretly pleased to have caught him looking at her, or his interpretation of her. It made her feel worthy of his skills. Perhaps it wasn't only her mother's financing that had made Fragonard interested in painting her.

At any rate, she was in a much better mood already and happily took her place on the stool.

Sabine noticed that the book was just where she had left it. She opened it to the page where she had stopped last time and started to read. By this point in the story, Candide had traveled all over the world, lost his teacher, Pangloss, and most recently been flogged and beaten, and was now being tended to by an old woman, who would take him to Cunégonde. Sabine was elated to discover that Cunégonde was alive!

Together, Candide, the old woman, and Cunégonde boarded a ship bound for South America. Sabine loved how fast the story moved. When the three of them arrived in Buenos Aires, Candide and Cunégonde planned to marry, but the governor of the city wished to marry Cunégonde. To Sabine's shock, Cunégonde accepted the proposal, as it would ensure her financial well-being.

Disappointed, Sabine put the book down and considered Cunégonde's situation. Candide had done so much for Cunégonde. He loved her so. Certainly, the governor wouldn't do the same or love her as much. *But,* Sabine thought, *what kind of life could she have with the poor Candide, anyway?* Maybe Sabine, too, would have agreed to marry the governor.

Sabine picked up the book to start reading again, then quickly put it down. "No, no, no," she said out loud. Candide had endured so much for the love of Cunégonde. She *must not* marry the governor. She must go to Candide. When Sabine realized she had started talking to herself, she looked up to find Fragonard behind his canvas smiling at her. She was utterly embarrassed.

"*Oh—pardon, monsieur!*" she cried, expecting him to be angry. He had been so cold to her last time, she assumed he would find an outburst like this tedious.

"That's all right. You must like the book, eh?" The artist seemed amused.

"Well, yes. Have you read it?" Sabine felt emboldened and decided to try and have a conversation with the painter. She so wanted to know more about him.

"Yes, I have read it. I'm sorry to tell you that I found the whole thing rather a bore." Fragonard had turned his back to his work as he talked. "This Voltaire is like all the rest of them—the bourgeoisie wishing things were different, that man could be in charge of his own destiny." Sabine had no idea what he was talking about. He continued: "Well, if there weren't a king telling everyone what to do, I'd be out of work, mademoiselle, so you can keep that book if you like. Consider it a gift from me."

"*Merci beaucoup.*" Sabine couldn't imagine that they were talking about the same book, but she pretended to understand what Monsieur Fragonard was saying and smiled knowingly at him. "Should I pick it up again now?"

"As a matter of fact, your part is finished."

"Really? Well, can I see the portrait then?" Sabine asked excitedly.

"If you don't mind, I'd rather you waited until it is complete. There are still some things I have to work on. You'll see it soon enough, though. I promise."

Sabine was disappointed, but she understood that he was an artist and wanted his work to be perfect— she appreciated that.

"Well, then, I suppose I should be on my way," she said, standing up. She walked toward the door and picked up her coat off the rack. She paused before walking down the steps and decided to be frank. "I realize my mother paid you to paint my portrait, monsieur," she said quickly, "but, well, no matter how it came to be, I'm just honored to have had it done by such an extraordinary artist."

Fragonard nodded, his eyes bright. "No, mademoiselle, the honor was mine. I would have painted it had she not offered me a *centime*, and I told her as much when I asked her if I could paint you. Enjoy the book."

Sabine was stunned. She walked over to the artist with a newfound confidence and held out her hand to him as she curtsied. He took it and kissed it, and she turned and walked out of the studio, Antoine trailing quickly behind her.

"Everything all right, mademoiselle? You look a bit sad." Antoine was so kind.

"I'm fine, Antoine. Let's just get home." Sabine wasn't sure if it was sadness she was feeling or deep, searing pain. Her mother had lied to her and for no reason. What kind of mother would rather have her daughter believe that she had to pay someone to paint her portrait than have her know the truth, that the artist would have done so for nothing? Margaux Durand, that was who, and Sabine felt sick to her stomach the whole way home.

"Antoine," Sabine called to her driver when they were nearing home.

"*Oui, mademoiselle?*" he answered.

"Are you and Cécile fond of each other?" The carriage stopped, and Antoine turned around. He seemed shaken.

"Mademoiselle, please don't tell Madame. I will break it off with Cécile. Please"—he was frantic, begging—"please. We would have to live on the streets."

Sabine was shocked. She hadn't meant to frighten Antoine. "No, Antoine! I would never tell." She was desperate for him to understand that she was not like her mother. "I would never want to interfere with you and Cécile. I don't even know why I asked. I just—" Sabine really didn't know why. Perhaps she wanted to live in someone else's life for a moment, because she was so miserable in her own. "I'm sorry. I think Cécile is lovely and that the two of you make a lovely couple. Forgive me for intruding. Please, carry on driving."

Antoine turned around, and once they arrived back at the Durand house, he and Sabine parted in silence.

Chapter Seven

That evening, Sabine couldn't rest. Between the incident with Jean-Philippe and the news Fragonard had delivered about her mother that morning, and then the way she had made Antoine feel, she was distraught. And besides all that, she kept going back to what Michel had said days before about her having no choices.

On some level, Sabine realized that she lived in a time and a place where many decisions would be made for her, but until Michel said it out loud, none of that had bothered her. Now, after her conversation with Élodie about Jean-Philippe, her confrontation with Jean-Philippe himself, and the response of her mother to all of it, Sabine realized that Michel was right.

But Sabine didn't want Michel to be right about anything. She wanted to want the same things Élodie did, wanted to be content having tea and dressing up for balls and the opera. If only those things could make her happy. Well, she had no choice. They would have to. For now, she had to stop thinking.

Sabine opened her door and felt the house at peace, so she stepped out into the hallway and headed for the outdoors. She didn't know it until she got there, but she was on her way to the pantry. Outside, the sky was turning dark blue and the air was winter-fresh. Sabine hadn't thought to take a wrap, but she didn't mind the chill one bit. Her long dress felt too heavy for her inside the house. Out here, she was comfortable. Perhaps in the very back of her mind, Sabine had half expected to find Michel leaning there as she had the other day, and was now a little disappointed that this wasn't the case. *But why would he be, anyway?* she thought. *He certainly has no reason to come here at this hour.*

Relieved just to be away from the house, she leaned against the side of the pantry, imitating Michel's pose. Sabine closed her eyes and pictured him. She admired his easy manner, she realized. She wished she could shed her corset and slump the way he did, relaxing his whole body against the building. She made a note to herself that one day or night, she would come out to this spot in her nightclothes just to feel what the outdoors felt like on her skin.

Sabine opened her eyes, and as if she had imagined him into being, Michel appeared.

"It's been quite a while since we've met here," he said to her, his eyes bright but his expression serious.

Sabine jumped. She scrambled for something to say and wondered what on earth had brought him to this place. She felt defensive. "Yes, but I didn't mean to come here," she replied, trying to convince herself that this was true. Michel had come face-to-face with her, and she was nervous. She stood up straight and clasped her clammy hands behind her back.

"Of course not. Why would you want to come and see me out by the pantry when you could be dreaming of Jean-Philippe in the warmth of your bedroom?" Michel joked.

"Why are you here?" she asked. "You haven't been to our house more than fifteen times in years, and suddenly you're here all the time." Sabine had, in the back of her mind, thought Michel might be coming to see her, but she knew it wasn't that.

"I just came from my mother's room. She needed some more of Madame Chaumont's tea for her cough," Michel said quickly. "Also," he added, "I had heard a little rumor about a misbehaving aristocrat and I thought I'd sweep in to see if all was well here." He actually had a shy look on his face, and Sabine's stomach flipped a little. *What's this?* she wondered. *How did Michel hear about Jean-Philippe?* And then she realized. Cécile, Antoine, and Michel had always been good friends. Clearly, that hadn't changed over the years.

"My, news—gossip, that is—certainly travels fast in your circle," Sabine said haughtily. Michel looked at her differently now, and Sabine knew she had offended him. As if being servants constituted a social circle. "Well, thank you for your concern, but I'm sure Jean-Philippe was just flirting." Michel looked away. "I do appreciate your looking out for me," Sabine added. She wanted him to know that it meant something to her that he cared. She unclasped her hands and used them to fuss with her skirt instead.

"Is that what he was doing? Flirting?" Michel asked dubiously. He took a small step away from Sabine, as if he knew he was making her nervous.

"Well, that's what my loving mother is comfortable believing, and I'm stuck with her, so I have to believe it, too. Anyway, where are you off to tonight?" Sabine asked, relaxing her pose as she tried to change the subject.

"I was going to the tavern with Étienne and some others." Michel paused as if he were deliberating about something. Then he continued: "Why don't you come with me?"

"Very funny, Michel." Sabine laughed at the mere thought of her telling her mother that she would be going out in the evening with Michel Bernard and Étienne Chaumont. It might almost be worth it just to see her face. "Thank you for asking me, but you and I both know that isn't possible."

"You don't have to tell your mother." Michel leaned in toward her as if he were telling her a secret. "We could sneak you out after supper. Cécile and Antoine are coming along as well. I'm sure they'll help us. That is, if you really wanted to come out." Michel grew serious.

"Then what, Michel? We traipse around Paris together and cause the biggest scandal in recent society history?" Sabine was again trying to convince herself that this would be a mistake.

"Well, fine, then. I just thought you'd like to

spend some time with interesting people for a change. I suppose I mistook your reading Voltaire for something more than it is. You're still a stickler for the rules about what's right and what isn't, eh?"

Michel must have been hurt to change his tone so fast, but Sabine had no better answer for him. She did believe in certain things. She had to. Like it or not, she could never go gallivanting around Paris with the likes of Michel. It simply wasn't proper.

"I just can't, Michel." She had to end this conversation.

"I'll be curious to see what kind of an effect Voltaire will have on these rules of yours, Sabine. Do let me know when you've finished the book," he said.

"What do you mean? As far as I can tell it is a love story." Sabine didn't understand what the fuss was about the book. She was pleased that Michel thought highly of her for reading it, but so far, she didn't really know why.

"I suppose it is a love story," Michel replied. "But

it's really about society and how willing people are to accept things as they are."

"What things?" Sabine asked. This must have been what Fragonard was talking about today, and she was glad to have Michel shed some light. She finally felt her body relax.

"You know—status, government, wealth . . ." Michel trailed off as Sabine furrowed her brow.

"I'm not sure what you mean," she said. "And anyway, that doesn't sound very interesting."

Michel shook his head and continued: "Well, the book is also about optimism. Pangloss teaches Candide that absolutely everything that happens is for the best, right?"

"Well, *I* think so!" Sabine usually thought of herself as an optimist. "Don't you, Michel? Do you think that's true?"

"I suppose I do. But Voltaire also seems to be saying that we are all free to determine the way things turn out in the world if we so choose. And I surely agree with that."

Sabine wasn't surprised to hear this. She understood now that Michel was looking for choices and that reading Voltaire had inspired him further. It did feel rather exciting to consider the idea of free will. Sabine then wondered if Michel identified with Candide the same way she saw pieces of herself in Cunégonde.

"Think of Mr. Benjamin Franklin and the Americans," Michel was saying. "They are not willing to accept the rules of the king of England, so they are rebelling. They are determining their own fate. Who knows if it will even work, but good for them for trying, eh? We ought to do just the same here."

Now Sabine was dismayed. "And rebel against *our* king? But why? I love France."

"Loving France doesn't mean leaving well enough alone, Sabine. Loving France can also mean helping it become a better country—one that values and regards all of its citizens equally. That's what the Americans want, after all. Why shouldn't *we*?"

"Surely all of the women who fawn over Mr. Franklin can't agree with him on these matters?" Sabine asked, frowning. "Why are they so enamored?" This was what she had asked Jean-Philippe, but he had chosen not to answer her.

"First of all, Mr. Franklin hasn't said anything about rebelling against our king, of course. In fact, our king is quite fond of him. And, as a result, so are all of—how did you put it?—your circle."

Sabine laughed an uncomfortable laugh. She had deserved that.

Michel continued: "Why does our king support the Americans, though? I don't really know. I suppose he thinks it would be good for France to forge a relationship with the new colonies. Not to mention the satisfaction of getting back at England! And I assume he doesn't think it is possible that such a thing could happen here. I'm quite sure that all of the women who adore Franklin so are in love with the idea of him—a scientist, a writer, a revolutionary.

These things make him a celebrity. No one around here is really thinking about his idea—"

"Least of all my mother," Sabine interrupted.

"Or Élodie, for that matter," Michel added, which annoyed Sabine—*and* reminded her that she and Michel were not friends. Élodie was her friend, and despite Sabine's reservations about Élodie's intentions, she felt she had to be loyal to her. Remembering what Élodie had said about Michel, Sabine decided to bid him good evening, lest he get the idea that the two of them were becoming friends once again.

"I should be going now," Sabine said suddenly, her posture stiff once more.

"Have I made you uncomfortable? I'm sorry." Michel was clearly being sarcastic, and Sabine felt again as if he were patronizing her. Their interactions always seemed to turn nasty, which reminded her that the class system made sense. This was the way it was meant to be: Sabine and Élodie going to the opera while Michel, Cécile, and Antoine drank wine in taverns.

"Good evening, Michel," Sabine said as she turned abruptly on her heel and headed back to the house in a hurry.

Chapter Eight

It took Sabine a long time to fall asleep after her encounter with Michel by the pantry. When she got back to her bedroom, she began to regret the way she had ended their conversation. Why had she become so defensive when he picked on Élodie? He was right, after all. Élodie hadn't ever cared much about ideas, but for that matter, neither had Sabine. But lately, and rather suddenly, Sabine had begun to think more about who she was, where she fit in, and what she believed in, and it was making her uncomfortable. Was it the book she was reading? Was it Franklin's arrival in Paris?

Or was it Michel?

Sabine had finally fallen asleep and thought she was dreaming when she heard a clicking sound at her window. She waited in her bed for a moment, thinking it might be a dream. But the noise persisted.

Then she thought it might be a tree branch or a bird, but when the noise still wouldn't relent, she wrapped herself in her robe and went to have a look. She cranked the window open and was immediately hit in the face with a pebble. Though the small pebble hadn't hurt her, she was stunned and drew her hands to her face dramatically.

When she looked down and saw Michel standing below her window with a handful of pebbles, she wasn't all that surprised.

"Michel! Are you mad? You hit me in the face!" Sabine cried. She was angry, but in spite of herself, she also thought it was a little bit funny and tried hard not to laugh.

"I'm sorry! You should have lit a candle. I couldn't see that you were there." She heard Michel stifling a chuckle—clearly he thought the encounter was funny, too—and she couldn't hold back any longer. She let out a loud laugh but put her hands over her mouth to quiet the noise.

"It's not funny," she said, still laughing.

"I know. It's not," Michel agreed, still laughing. "Anyway, I'm glad I got your attention. Sabine, you have to come with me."

"Now? It's ten o'clock at night."

"Madame Chaumont is hosting a salon, and we're invited. Put something on and let's go. I'll meet you by the horses." And he was gone.

Even though she knew it was improper to go out in the middle of the night with Michel, Sabine had to admit she was intrigued. She had heard about the salons—the late-night gatherings hosted by intellectuals—members of the bourgeoisie—where they talked about politics and art and philosophy. Sabine liked that women usually hosted them, chose the topics for conversation, and moderated them, too. Plus, one never knew who might be there.

Sabine quickly got her corset on and put on the same dress she had worn to be painted by Fragonard, in case there really was someone important there. She couldn't help thinking that despite her mother's objections to salons—she thought they weren't elegant—she would be mortified if Sabine weren't properly attired for the event.

As she tiptoed out of her room, down the stairs and out through the kitchen door, her insides were churning. Who was this girl running out of the house with the help in the middle of the night? What was she thinking? She decided *not* to think but just go and do, for once.

She found Michel standing next to a saddled horse. "How's your face?" he asked, smiling.

"That's funny, Michel," she said. "Do let me know how you think I should explain the bump to Mother tomorrow." Her cheek actually stung a little, but Sabine didn't want Michel to know he had hurt her at all. She realized she didn't want him to feel bad about it.

"Tell her you were beating yourself up about the way you treated Jean-Philippe," Michel suggested as he hopped up on the horse. Sabine looked up at him as if he were crazy. He did seem a little crazy to her tonight. "Come on, take my hand," Michel added.

"You want me to get up on that horse with you?" Now Sabine *knew* he was crazy.

"Sorry I couldn't take out the carriage for you, darling," Michel said in a mocking tone.

Sabine wouldn't have it. She grabbed his hand and hoisted herself onto the horse, flipping one leg over to straddle it. She knew she should ride sidesaddle and that this pose wasn't ladylike, but suddenly she didn't care. The horse trotted in the direction of the Chaumonts' home, and the wind put redness on her face that she hoped would cover the blush she felt fill her cheeks as she held her arms tightly around Michel's waist.

When they arrived, she realized that although she had been to Dr. Chaumont's office, she had never been to the Chaumont home. But Sabine liked it right away. From Madame Chaumont's reception—she opened the door herself!—to the candles flickering all around the house, Sabine noticed how much warmer everything felt than in her own home. Less fussy. The velvet on the settee was worn down in spots, as if people actually sat there. In Sabine's house, a settee was strictly for show.

Madame Chaumont showed Sabine and Michel to the long table, where Étienne was already seated. He got up to shake Michel's hand and bow to Sabine, which Sabine, despite her objections to Étienne, actually found rather charming. There were quite a lot of people milling about, taking their seats, shaking hands, patting each other heartily on the back. Everything here was so earnest, and Sabine found the whole scene enchanting.

Sabine noticed how differently the table was set from her mother's table. The china patterns were mixed, and stocky candles of all different heights sat alongside fresh-cut flowers in all different shades of orange, yellow, lavender, and fuchsia in cut crystal vases. These were not grand arrangements like the ones her mother had anguished over before last week's ball. They were simple and bold, and they were even more stunning as a result. The chairs at the table were mismatched, too, and Sabine couldn't help thinking that her mother would scoff at the whole scene. Sabine, on the other hand, thought it was exquisite.

She took her seat next to Michel and waited for everyone else to sit as well. She was still taking it all in, watching the guests mingle and slowly find their way to their individual seats, when she spotted a man who looked familiar to her. Sitting there in a fur cap, he looked awfully funny. Who wore a fur cap in Paris? But Sabine was sure she had seen him before.

As Madame Chaumont called the salon to attention, Sabine studied the man closely. He had long, straggly hair, and he wore a very simple brown suit without any fancy needlework on the coat, just plain silver buttons and a flowing white blouse with a loosely tied cravat. But it was the round glasses perched on his nose that stopped Sabine. Suddenly, she couldn't breathe. Of course she had seen him before—his likeness was stamped on the snuff box in her father's study, and his portrait hung over their mantelpiece. Benjamin Franklin was here at this very table!

Michel must have noticed this just then, too, because he nudged her arm at precisely the same time she went to nudge his and they knocked elbows rather hard as a result. Sabine surely *was* going to wake up bruised tomorrow morning, but, oh, it would be worth it. And it would remind her that this night was real!

The conversation started then, and Madame Chaumont introduced all the people at the table, including Sabine. At this, Sabine was startled—she wasn't an important guest. Michel was included in the introductions as well. It felt as if there were no classes, no divisions, at the table, and Sabine was thrilled to be a part of it. When Mr. Franklin was introduced, the whole table clapped and cheered.

Someone spoke up from the other end of the table—it was Dr. Chaumont: "Dr. Franklin," he said, "we hear you have a little war on your hands over there. Do tell us what all the fuss is about, eh?"

Though it was Franklin who was to address the crowd, it was Sabine who had butterflies flitting around in her gut as Franklin pondered his response. But the American showed no nervousness at all. All eyes were on him as he stood up, using his knuckles to lean forward on the table. The way he looked around at all of them made Sabine feel as if he were about to tell them a story.

"Glad you asked, sir, and I'd be happy to oblige," Mr. Franklin stated. "This little war you speak of is actually rather momentous. We have some grand ideas over there in the colonies, and I'm sure that some of you in France might agree with them."

"Tell us, sir. We'd all love to hear." Madame Chaumont spoke with a broad smile, her chin resting on her hands, which were folded around a goblet of red wine.

Franklin gave an easy wink at his hostess that would have made Sabine melt had he looked that way at her. She was beginning to understand the adoration.

"You see," he went on, "the boatloads of people who went over to the New World—they were *starting* a new world. And for a while, they were content to be a part of the most powerful kingdom in Europe." He paused and looked around as if he were expecting the crowd to groan. And groan they did. Sabine was happy to join in when she saw she would be the only one holding back. Groaning at a dinner party—how rude! How wonderful!

"Well, they were, of course!" Franklin was clearly amused by this public scoffing at the English throne. "But over time, they . . . *we* made that land our own, and we came to believe that we deserved to be in charge of our own destiny. After all, the king of England doesn't know our land. He doesn't know our schools, our shops, our churches, or our libraries. And perhaps most important, he doesn't know our way of life. We had become a different nation. We were England no longer. So when people realized that someone else was making decisions that affected their lives—the life of the farmer, the merchant, the schoolteacher—well, that farmer, that merchant, and that schoolteacher, they thought, *Now, that isn't quite right, is it?* So we got together and decided to try it another way. And that's what we're doing now—fighting to try it another way, the way we think it will work best. Because isn't it true that the true source of any government's power is the consent of the people it seeks to govern? That is what guided us when we wrote our Declaration of Independence—this truth, the self-evident truth, that all men are created equal and are endowed with certain unalienable rights of life, liberty, and the pursuit of happiness. And what does the king of England know, how *could* he know, about a Pennsylvania farmer's pursuit of happiness?"

Franklin's delivery was perfect, and Sabine was completely overwhelmed. Here was this tall, slightly pudgy around the middle, bespectacled man, who commanded the floor as if he were a king himself, and yet he was asking the king of France to support America in overthrowing the king of England—what bravado, indeed.

As the night went on, so did the dialogue. "But Dr. Franklin, we are a monarchy here, and many believe it should stay that way. Why would our king ever support the Americans?" Franklin easily made the case that if the bourgeoisie would support the cause, so would the king, for Louis XVI was already losing their trust and support. Sabine wasn't quite clear about what this meant until the conversation turned to French politics and the crowd got a bit more raucous as they discussed putting an end to the monarchy. She found herself a little angry at this suggestion, but Franklin quoted a man named Thomas Paine: "The trade of governing has always been monopolized by the most ignorant and the most rascally individuals of mankind." Was he actually calling the king "rascally"? *What a scandal!* Sabine thought. But as she listened—"We should take a lesson from the Americans! . . ." "We should rise up! . . ." "We should listen to Rousseau and Voltaire, let any man become what he's capable of!"—she started to understand at last what Monsieur Fragonard had meant, what Michel had meant, when they had talked about *Candide*. It wasn't just a love story at all.

Madame Chaumont interrupted the conversation just then to serve the meal. It was country fare— roasted duck, a creamy potato gratin, and an onion and tomato *tian*. The food warmed up the room, and everyone settled into more casual conversation. And as the night wound down, Sabine was surprised when Michel spoke up just as the people at the table began to disperse.

"Mr. Franklin, if I may," he said, and paused. Franklin nodded a vigorous *yes* as he took a swig of his wine. Michel continued: "I quite admire what you're doing over there. In fact, yours is a fight I'd be proud to be a part of. Maybe if it works for the Americans, France will follow your lead." He spoke with tremendous confidence. Franklin slid his chair back, got up out of it, and walked toward Michel.

"We'd be glad to have you. Michel, right?" he asked as he held out his hand.

"*Oui, monsieur*," Michel said as he shook Franklin's hand. "Michel Bernard." Just then, Mr. Franklin was whisked away from them by Dr. Chaumont. It was then that Sabine looked at the clock and realized it was after two o'clock in the morning!

Soon, the party broke up, and Sabine and Michel kissed their hosts good-bye and set out for home. After a recap of all the wonderful highlights of the evening, they rode the rest of the way in silence. When they arrived home, Michel helped Sabine off the horse.

Face-to-face with Michel now, Sabine realized she had a question for him. "Did you mean it when you told Mr. Franklin you'd like to be a part of their revolution? Would you really go there and fight with them?" she whispered.

Michel didn't even pause. "I would go in an instant," he said.

Sabine's heart dropped when he said this. Suddenly the thought of Michel leaving—however unrealistic—saddened her. And yet at the same time, she realized she was proud that she had gone with Michel to the Chaumonts', proud that she had sat at the same table as Mr. Benjamin Franklin, and proud that she knew someone who would go off to another land and risk his life for something he believed in.

"Are you glad you came?" Michel asked softly.

She wasn't sure what to say. Standing before her was the boy with whom she had spent her childhood. In those days, she would come into the house, flushed from running around outside all afternoon when she should have been practicing her posture. Tonight she should have been practicing again to be obedient and refined, practicing loving someone she couldn't possibly ever love. And again, she was flushed—from being outside, from riding on horseback with the boy whose grip made her feel steady as a child and whose very presence now made her queasy with aspiration. He made her want to escape, to rebel against everything she knew. She knew this was the beginning of a revolution indeed. But all she could say was, "This was the best night of my life, Michel." That was the only answer she could give at the moment. If she had started to say something else, to really let out all that was brewing inside her, well, she might never have gone back inside. And she had to go back. She gave Michel a quick kiss and then ran toward the door, her heart pounding out of her chest.

Chapter Nine

Sabine spent most of Saturday recovering from the night before. Though she wasn't physically bruised from all of her mishaps with Michel, the evening had certainly left its mark. Lying in her bedroom, Sabine read *Candide* to distract herself from thinking too much about Michel. Besides, after the previous night's discussion, she was finally beginning to understand that Voltaire had more to say than she had originally thought. She hadn't known that people like Rousseau and Voltaire were trying to get people to think about France the way the revolutionaries in America thought. This, she had gathered the night before, was their true purpose.

Sabine knew she should have been primping for the opera, but she wanted to finish her book. As she read, she was thinking about what Michel had told her about the book, and about everything happening for the best. She read so fast that she felt like she was skipping sentences just because she was so eager to find out what happened. Though she loved the writing, it was really the plot that stirred her. Would these characters find love and happiness? And if so, how?

Candide, having lost Cunégonde once again, found himself in the land of El Dorado, a place where gold and jewels are available to everyone, but have no value. It was a utopia, where there was no crime and no conflict. Sabine thought it sounded divine. But Candide decided to load up with gold and jewels and go in search of Cunégonde once again. Along the way, though, when his fortune was stolen from him, Candide began to feel pessimistic for the first time. He continued to think he had no control over matters such as these. But then, when he was able to recover some of his fortune later, he took it as proof that there was justice in the world. Sabine, on the other hand, was beginning to find Candide himself a bit tedious. *It's one thing to be optimistic and hope for the best,* she thought, *but you have to take some responsibility for the way things turn out.*

The pages were flying by, and Sabine could sense that the book was coming to an end, both by the pace of the writing and by the waning thickness of the pages in her right hand. She was drained and glad to be interrupted by a rap on her door.

"Yes?" Sabine called to the door.

"May I come in?" It was Margaux, and Sabine was shocked that she had not simply barged in.

"Yes, of course, Mother." Sabine assumed she must be up to something.

"Darling," her mother began, entering the room. "I wanted to help you get ready for the opera. You should wear something special. You never know whom you'll see."

Like Jean-Philippe, Sabine thought. "Thank you, Mother." Sabine decided to take the opportunity to talk to her mother about some of the things she had been thinking about. "You know, I was just wondering, why do you admire Mr. Franklin so?"

Margaux looked at Sabine with a puzzled expression. "Well, because he is a man of great achievement, of course. He is a scientist and writer and he also has strong moral values. You know all of this, Sabine. Why are you asking such a question?"

"I ask because it occurred to me that he is leading the colonists in a rebellion against the king of England. I can't imagine you would follow should someone here lead a rebellion against our king."

"First of all, the king of England is a fool. Second, France is lovely as it is, no?"

"Well, yes, I think it is. But maybe others don't. Maybe others think they should be able to determine their own fate and that our system doesn't allow for that. In a way, that is what the colonists are doing. They are starting fresh so that everyone has an equal chance at success. I think this is what Mr. Franklin stands for, not our way of life really." Sabine couldn't believe she was saying these things to her mother and braced herself for the response. If her mother only knew that she had sat at the same table as Mr. Franklin discussing—well, listening to others discuss—these very things, it would have taken smelling salts to revive her.

"Where did you get this nonsense from?" Margaux snapped. "In France, where you are born is where you stay. The colonists are starting a new country, and they are free to do it their way. Things needn't change here and they won't." She headed for Sabine's dressing room.

"Then why do you care if I marry Jean-Philippe?" Sabine blurted out. "Won't it help our status if I do?"

"Oh, Sabine!" her mother shouted from the closet. Then she emerged with Sabine's least favorite dress. "Enough of this now. The revolution of the colonies affects us only because it will help our country and hurt England. That's good enough for me, and it should be for you, too. And by the way, our family status is just fine. Your father is a prince. Marrying into the de Croy family would simply merge two very fine families."

Sabine knew that her mother just couldn't admit that the Durands were not nearly as "fine" as the de Croy family—and that this marriage would make her feel more legitimate. Sabine thought for a moment that she might actually respect her mother if she would just be honest with herself and with Sabine. If she would just admit that she was insecure about her status and that only being a part of the aristocracy made her feel important, Sabine could relate to that in some way. But her conniving made Sabine angry instead.

Madame Durand finally left Sabine to bathe and said she'd return to help her dress. Sabine hoped she'd leave her in peace. She enjoyed her bath, where her mind was free to drift. She thought about what Mr. Franklin, in his simple suit and fur cap, had said about the Americans building their world from the ground up—the shops, the schools, the homes. She closed her eyes and let herself imagine being there, walking the cobblestone streets, wearing layered cotton skirts and old, worn lace-up boots, carrying a bushel of vegetables home from the street market. There was dirt on her shoes but a smile on her face. She was smiling in this imaginary picture, and she was smiling in the tub. *What am I doing?* she wondered. *Why does the life of a colonist appeal to me?* Why, when she had everything a girl could want, would she opt for less?

Perhaps it wasn't less. Perhaps it was more.

Her mother never did return, but Brigitte did. When Sabine was powdering her nose, she noticed

Brigitte in the mirror and was disturbed. Her governess was pale and drawn.

"Brigitte? Are you all right?" Sabine asked in the mirror.

"I just can't seem to get rid of this cold—that's all." Brigitte's voice sounded weak and shaky.

"I think you'd better have some tea and stay in bed. I can finish getting ready myself."

"Yes, I think I'll do that," Brigitte answered with a sigh.

Sabine was upset that Brigitte had agreed. In the first place, she wanted to talk to her about Jean-Philippe and Élodie and all of her problems (though she could never tell her anything about Michel or her night at the Chaumonts'). And second, the fact that Brigitte agreed to go meant that she was sicker than she wanted to admit. Brigitte absolutely never took a rest, and she never, ever left Sabine to dress herself.

On her way out of the room, Brigitte squeezed Sabine's shoulder. "You're lovely, Sabine. Enjoy yourself tonight. And don't worry—when you get home, come get me, and we'll make sense of all the nonsense."

Sabine smiled. Brigitte had been saying this to her since she was a little girl. Whenever she got upset, Brigitte would get Sabine to talk about what was bothering her. Somehow, calling it nonsense made Sabine feel better. Brigitte had always made her feel better. Even now, when Sabine hadn't really told Brigitte anything about how she'd been feeling, Brigitte seemed to know she was bothered and wanted to help.

Sabine felt lighter knowing she and Brigitte would have a chat when she got home. In the meantime, at least she had the opera to look forward to. She always had a marvelous time at the opera.

Chapter Ten

The Fourniers' box was perfectly positioned to look out at both the stage and the audience. Sabine's family didn't have their own seats. This was one thing Madame Durand hadn't made a point of. Though she might pretend otherwise in the company of those who were, she wasn't a fan of the opera. But Sabine was, and she was thrilled to be in one of the best seats in the house tonight.

They were early, so they had some time to watch the room. Sabine and Élodie sat side by side, and as usual, they commented on just about everyone they could see. Sabine was still feeling cool toward her friend and was glad they were talking about other people's business. She knew she couldn't tell Élodie anything about Michel or the salon at the Chaumonts' and wondered if the two girls were really friends at all. What kind of friends could they be if Sabine couldn't tell Élodie about the most important thing that had ever happened to her?

Élodie's parents were there, and they were charming and warm to Sabine. Madame Fournier even suggested that Sabine and her mother join them for tea next week. Sabine found this a little odd since it was obvious to her and to most everyone else that women like Madame Fournier almost *never* had tea with women like Madame Durand. True, the families were friendly, but there had never been a close friendship between the two women. Attending the same events, making conversation at a supper party, that was one thing. Tea in someone's home was quite another. Margaux would be ecstatic. Sabine wondered what had prompted this invitation.

At a lull in the conversation, Sabine told Élodie

that she was reading *Candide* and how wrapped up in the book she had become. She decided this was a good way to talk to her friend about some of the things she had been thinking about without actually telling her about her late-night rendezvous with Michel.

"Do you believe in free will, Élodie?" Sabine asked, leaning back in her seat.

"What do you mean?" Élodie furrowed her brow.

"Do you believe we have any control over what happens in the world? In our lives?"

"Sabine, wherever do you come up with thoughts like these? I don't know. I suppose we have as much control as we want to have."

Sabine considered this. It actually made sense to her, and for a moment, it made her proud to have defended Élodie to Michel.

"You haven't told me about your tea with Jean-Philippe, Sabine. Was it divine?" Élodie was always a master at changing the subject.

"I'm not sure you'll like what I have to say, Élodie. He was just awful. He actually grabbed my wrist and wouldn't let go until—" Sabine paused. She didn't want to tell Élodie about Cécile. Elodie, too, had rules and clung fiercely to them.

"Oh, Sabine, come now. I'm sure he was just being firm about his interest in you. Consider yourself lucky to have someone feel so passionate about you!"

Now it was Sabine who wanted to change the subject. "Isn't that the marquis de Lafayette?" she asked when she spotted an acquaintance of theirs in a box across the theater.

"Why, yes, it is," Élodie said. "I hear he's gone perfectly mad. He actually wants to go to the *colonies* to help them fight their revolution. I believe the king is rather perturbed about it."

"Really? But how brave of him. Someone like him—well, like us—risking so much. I wonder why." Sabine thought it was wonderful that the marquis wanted to go. She hoped he would just so she could daydream about his journey. Daydreams were all she had right now.

As Sabine was thinking about Lafayette, she noticed the empty seats in the Fourniers' box and wondered who else would be joining them. She never got a chance to ask because at that moment Jean-Philippe and Paul de Croy showed up.

The entire Fournier family was instantly up out of their seats with delight. Sabine was confused. Had this been planned? Her manners told her to get up, but she did so reluctantly and slowly.

Jean-Philippe quickly took her hand. "No, mademoiselle, don't get up," he murmured, and he kissed her hand gently as if he were the kindest, shyest young man in Paris. Sabine was not fooled. And she was not happy with her friend for setting her up in this way. Alas, she had no choice. The music was starting, and the lights had dimmed.

Sabine felt claustrophobic sitting next to Jean-Philippe. She lifted her opera glasses to her eyes and looked to the stage for an escape. She tried hard not to think about her company and tried even harder not to think about the fact that her dearest friend had betrayed her and tricked her into this awful evening. Tears welled in her eyes as she watched. The music carried her away as it vibrated in her chest. It was Italian, and it was gorgeous. It occurred to her that she would like to see an opera made of *Candide*. It was romantic and tragic, dramatic and passionate. It would be perfect.

By the time intermission came, Sabine had almost forgotten her circumstances. But she was quickly reminded when the lights came up and Jean-Philippe turned to her.

"Sabine, you should know that my parents have granted me the privilege of marrying the girl of my choosing."

"How lovely for you, Jean-Philippe."

"And how lovely for you, Sabine. I've chosen you, and your parents have agreed. We're going the old-fashioned route, my dear. Our parents have made an arrangement for us to be married." He said this with such enthusiasm that Sabine thought for sure he was joking. He had to be.

"An arranged marriage? Are you out of your mind, monsieur?" Sabine didn't know if she should be outraged or amused. There was absolutely no way her parents would do this to her. Even her mother would think this was too old-fashioned.

"No, Sabine. I'm not at all out of my mind— although some might think so, since I'm making it my business to marry you. I've decided you're just the kind of challenge I'd enjoy. I think we'll have a good old time as husband and wife. My parents are a bit dismayed at having to join with your family by marriage, as you can imagine, but I've told them having the Durands in the family will only make us more interesting, don't you think?"

Sabine was horrified. This couldn't be happening. She turned to Élodie to tell her the awful news and found her friend beaming at her.

"What on earth are you smiling at, Élodie?" Sabine demanded. "Have you heard this?"

"Yes, of course. And guess what, darling! Paul has asked me to marry him. We're going to be sisters!" Élodie wrapped Sabine in a hug so tight, Sabine could hardly breathe. And when she let go, she found she *still* couldn't breathe and the whole room was spinning. She felt herself slip off her seat and fall to the floor.

Moments later, Sabine awoke to a crowd of faces hovering over her. For a minute, she had forgotten where she was and thought it had all been a dream. But then she saw Jean-Philippe and Paul and Élodie and their worried but amused expressions and decided to close her eyes again. Her heart was breaking. If she kept her eyes closed, maybe the tears wouldn't roll out.

Sabine let the group help her up and guide her to the Fourniers' carriage, which would take her home. She thought she would be going alone and that the others would stay for the second part of the opera, but apparently Élodie was coming with her. Jean-Philippe kissed her hand and helped her into the carriage. She winced at his touch.

"I'll pay you a visit tomorrow, Sabine." Jean-Philippe said as the door closed. "Oh, and do tell your mother that you'll all join us for supper next Saturday evening to celebrate the engagement."

Sabine rolled her eyes.

Élodie saw this and said glibly, "You're not going to faint again, are you, Sabine?"

"How could you do this to me?" Sabine asked Élodie as the carriage rolled away. "You know how I feel about Jean-Philippe. You set me up." As she said this, she felt herself choking back tears, and finally, she couldn't hold them in any longer. "You pretended to understand the other day, and then you invited me to the opera, knowing that the de Croys would be joining us," she said, crying. "Did you also know that we were going to be married, whether I like it or not?" She paused as something occurred to her. "What am I saying? Of course you did. You were having tea with Mother the day I came in from the rain."

Élodie was looking at Sabine with surprise, but

Sabine knew the truth now. Élodie had never really been her friend. "All those times you let me believe you understood about my mother," Sabine continued, choking up. "You laughed with me about her. But all along you were plotting with her, plotting to make me unhappy just so the two of you could get what you wanted."

"Is it so terrible that I wanted the two of us to be sisters?" Élodie asked. "My God, Sabine. What did you think, anyway? Who did you think you would marry? You wouldn't have loved anyone you could have married."

"How do you know that? How could you possibly know that?" Sabine cried.

"Because not one of them is Michel," Élodie replied.

Sabine was speechless. What could she say? She wasn't even sure if it was true, but she certainly couldn't say it *wasn't*.

The carriage pulled up to the Durand home, and the driver came around to escort Sabine. As she stepped out, Élodie touched her shoulder. She looked into Sabine's eyes and whispered, "Sabine, darling, what did you honestly expect?"

Sabine didn't know. But she said, "I expected my dresses to always be chosen for me—my breakfast, lunch, and dinner, too. I also expected Mother to love me just a little, and some kindness from you, and yes, Elodie, to have a say in whom I marry. Beyond that, I hadn't given it much thought."

With that, Sabine hopped out of the carriage, waved off the driver, and took herself to her front door. She paused before heading up her front steps. She heard a rustling and low voices down the side-door path, so she headed in that direction instead. She didn't want to face her mother just yet, so she followed the sounds. At the end of the path, she found Cécile and Antoine, holding hands and heading away from the house.

"Cécile!" Sabine shouted in a whisper.

Cécile seemed to jump out of her skin at this, and she turned around, letting go of Antoine's hand abruptly. "Mademoiselle!" Cécile whispered back. "I was just telling Antoine that I—"

Sabine interrupted Cécile's attempt to explain herself. "Please, Cécile. It's all right. I told Antoine, and I am telling you, I would never tell my mother. In fact, I was wondering where you were off to. I'd rather do just about anything other than go inside right now."

Sabine looked at Antoine and Cécile hopefully as they exchanged puzzled looks with each other. "You want to come with us, mademoiselle?" Cécile asked, practically stuttering. "Are you sure? I mean, is that proper, or, um, surely Madame Durand wouldn't approve?" Cécile clearly had no idea what to say. It seemed as if she felt responsible for Sabine and that she was trying to talk her out of going with them.

"Cécile," Sabine said gently, trying to relate to her, "I want to go with you. If it's a tavern, that's all right. Please don't be afraid of my mother. I'll handle her." *Besides,* Sabine thought, *Mother won't have any idea where I am. As far as she knows, I'm still at the opera.*

"Well, if you say so, mademoiselle," Cécile said, her tone still loaded with doubt. "We *are* going to the tavern."

Antoine whispered something to Cécile then, and Cécile looked Sabine up and down. "Perhaps you want to go change your clothes first, mademoiselle."

Sabine understood their concern—she would certainly stand out in her opera dress. But she had no choice. She couldn't possibly go inside and change and make it outside again without her mother knowing.

"Well," Sabine said a little self-consciously, "I think this will have to do, Cécile. I'm not sure anything I have would be right anyway. Now," she said, threading her arm through Cécile's, "let's get out of here."

Chapter Eleven

They walked a while until they reached a tavern Sabine had to have passed by all the time and yet, until this moment, she had never noticed it. Sabine thought she'd walk into a loud, raucous place, but the whole scene was rather tame. In fact, she wished it had been much louder, so she wouldn't have been so noticeable. The place quieted all the way down when people started to notice her.

"The princess is slumming, is she?" a man asked. Sabine could smell the alcohol oozing from this man's pores, and she felt a lump start to form in her throat. This place wasn't for her. She heard jeers of solidarity as she walked by this man—clearly he had a lot of friends. But she stayed focused on the backs of Cécile and Antoine, who were headed toward the rear of the place. Another man cut her off before she could catch up to them, though, and she felt the lump rise.

"*La petite princesse,*" the man sneered. "You're scared stiff. Perhaps you should have left your corset at the door." He laughed and coughed so that his spittle hit Sabine in the face.

She was disgusted and feeling as if she should leave, but something inside her kept her firmly there. She leaned into the man and poked his large belly. "Is it that you wanted to borrow it, sir?" she said with a half smile, loud enough for his drinking buddies to hear.

At that, the place erupted, and the men cleared a path for her. She was proud, but mostly relieved, as she approached Cécile and Antoine, who were visibly stunned. Then she heard the sound of loud clapping coming from behind them. It was Michel and Étienne, who were already seated and who had apparently witnessed her confrontation as well.

"Brava!" Étienne hooted.

"You *are* a bit overdressed, Sabine," Michel chided her. "This place is nice, I suppose, but not that nice." He was smiling at her.

That smile. Sabine, who was all puffed up from her confrontation with the drunkard, fell to pieces inside now. If Michel had stood up right then and taken her in his arms and pulled her close, she would have touched his face and kissed it one thousand times. And she would have let him kiss hers. It was Michel's kind, tortured face and not Jean-Philippe's sharp entitled one that Sabine had dreamed about not just in her sleep but when she was wide awake. It was his face that had kept Sabine sane for as long as she could remember. And it was his face that would keep her going now, in the wake of the news she had received at the opera. But he didn't stand up, and he didn't take her in his arms. So there would not be one thousand kisses tonight, not even one. There would only be this awkward moment—Sabine standing there with no chair in which to sit.

Sabine came back to reality suddenly. She wasn't sure what to do next. No one got up for her. At last sensing the problem, Étienne and Michel popped out of their seats, and Étienne took a chair from the neighboring table and gestured that it was for Sabine. Sabine was relieved to sit down—it enabled her to escape the glances of everyone in the room.

"Étienne," Antoine said, "You made it out. I wasn't sure you'd be here after the last time." They all laughed, and Sabine wondered what had happened.

"Étienne's father discovered him here, and let's just say he wasn't pleased," Cécile explained, taking a big gulp of the wine Antoine had poured out of a carafe on the table.

Sabine looked at Étienne. Apparently the two of them had more in common than Sabine would have ever believed.

"So, your parents don't know you're here either?" she asked him.

"No," Étienne said. "A tavern is one thing, but this particular tavern is quite another. You know, it's one thing to bring a peasant into a bourgeois place—that is civilized and interesting. But for me to walk into this place, well, that's just taking the whole charade a bit too far."

This was fascinating to Sabine. Here she had thought the Chaumonts were so very progressive, but like everyone else in Paris, it seemed, they had their own rules, too. *Be friendly with the help if you want. Bring them for supper. Just don't have supper in their part of town.* Brigitte had been right. Michel probably was a cause for the Chaumonts, and nothing more. And yet not to Étienne. He had taken a risk to be here with his friend's friends, and suddenly Sabine admired Étienne a great deal.

She looked at Michel, then, who seemed a little hurt at the idea that the Chaumonts didn't find him perfect company for their son. "What can I say?" he said, noting Sabine's look. "I cause trouble in every class!" He took a swig of his wine and let out a big, exasperated noise. It made Sabine want to make a noise, too.

She let out a big sigh, bigger than any she had ever sighed before, and started to laugh wildly. What was this? Who was she? She had no idea anymore, but she was here to find out.

As the night went on and Sabine settled in to the place, she found that she was the most relaxed she'd been in a very long time. The five of them shared wine, told stories, and laughed at various antics going on around the tavern all night long. Time seemed to be standing still. Without all the pretense of her everyday life, Sabine liked herself better. This group laughed at her sense of humor and would probably never refer to her actions as antics. In the few hours she spent with them, she felt a closeness—a bond—that she had yet to really feel with anyone, even Élodie. She caught a glimpse of herself in the mirror that hung on the wall behind

Étienne and Michel, and she noticed that she looked pink and alive. She felt no sadness looking at herself right then, none at all.

At a pause in the conversation, Cécile put a hand on Sabine's shoulder. "We really ought to be getting you back now, Mademoiselle. I'm sure the opera has long been over, and besides, we have a big day tomorrow."

What does she mean? Sabine wondered, looking puzzled at her new friend.

"Madame Durand asked me to escort you to the seamstress to have a fitting for your dress."

"What dress?" Sabine asked.

"Why, your wedding dress, mademoiselle! Aren't you just thrilled? I was so delighted when Madame asked me to go with you in Brigitte's place, what with Brigitte feeling so under the weather and all. . . ." Cécile trailed off when she noticed that the table was quiet and Sabine had gone pale.

"You knew about this wedding as well?" Sabine asked Cécile.

"Well, I . . . yes." Cécile struggled to answer. She didn't understand that Sabine had only found out about her engagement tonight, and she certainly couldn't know how devastating the news was.

Meanwhile, Sabine caught Michel's eye, but he quickly looked down at his nearly empty cup. "Well, then, let's get the princess home," Michel said too loudly, giving away his irritation.

"Michel," Sabine started to explain, "I didn't know anything about this. You know it's not—*he's* not . . ."

"Now, now, Sabine," Michel said as if he were speaking to a child. "In time, you'll get used to the idea, and our night here in the tavern will become ancient history—a last hurrah, if you will, slumming it with the help." He stood and threw some coins on the table. "Glad we could be of service, mademoiselle," he said, and headed for the door.

Étienne got up to go after him, waving a quick good-bye to the others. Antoine, Cécile, and Sabine got up in unison as well, and Sabine followed the two of them out of the tavern with her eyes glued to the floor. They walked home in silence, and when they got to the front door, Cécile took Sabine's hand and squeezed it.

"I didn't know you didn't want to marry Monsieur de Croy," Cécile said, looking at Sabine. "I mean, I saw the way he treated you the other day, but I told myself it was a quarrel and nothing more. I can't imagine having to marry someone I didn't love, mademoiselle."

"I can't imagine wanting to marry anyone at all, Cécile," Sabine said before she could even think. But it was true. "You'd best go in the side entrance, or Mother will have a fit," she said, turning to the front door. Sabine waited until Cécile and Antoine had disappeared before opening the door.

When she came in, her mother was pacing the sitting room angrily. "Where have you been?" she demanded when she saw Sabine.

Sabine studied her mother's face as she waited a minute to answer her. Her expression wasn't concerned as someone else's mother might be. *Is everything all right?* another mother might ask. But Margaux's expression asked one question only: *What did you do to embarrass me?*

"Don't even answer. I don't actually want to know. I was sitting here thinking of my only daughter enjoying herself at the opera, when Jean-Philippe showed up at our door out of concern that you might be ill. Imagine my surprise when he told me you had left with Élodie at intermission."

Sabine was shocked. She hadn't counted on this.

"Well, don't you worry, my darling," her mother said huffily. "I told him you were in fact feeling a bit ill and had turned in early. And here I sit now, facing a girl who has the blush of wine on her cheeks."

"I fainted, and there was concern that I might be ill, so I did come home with Élodie. I just didn't come inside." Sabine took a matter-of-fact approach.

"Were you overheated?" her mother asked, as if she might have fainted due to something other than the horrible and surprising news Jean-Philippe had delivered. "Wasn't Jean-Philippe there to tend to you?"

"Why, yes, Mother. He was there. In fact, he had just told me the news of our arranged engagement when I thought I might be sick. Imagine how embarrassing that was! There I was, having just found out I was to be married, from the man I am to marry, and I fall ill!" Sabine was shouting and gesturing in grand fashion as if she were performing in a play.

"Leave it to you to be dramatic, Sabine. I must say, though, I am surprised that Jean-Philippe would tell you the news like that. We had discussed a more romantic proposal. Well, anyway, Jean-Philippe will be coming here tomorrow to make it official."

"You had discussed a more romantic proposal?" Sabine was disgusted. Apparently, she had discussed a lot of things with a lot of people—just not with her. "I'm going to bed." She turned to go up the stairs, then looked back at Margaux. "Mother, I will not marry him." She said, and she walked calmly up the stairs. *I will not,* she thought.

"Oh, yes, you will, Sabine," her mother countered, standing at the bottom of the stairs. "You will marry him, and perhaps he will discipline you better than I ever could."

Sabine could not sleep. She kept having imaginary conversations with her mother and Jean-Philippe— conversations where she said just the right thing in just the right way. She was always so well-spoken in her own head, but when the real confrontation came, she would shake inside and out and stumble over the words.

When Sabine couldn't stand to think about everything for one more minute, she picked up *Candide.* She had to finish it once and for all. She flipped the last pages fast. She just wanted to find out what happened, how it all would end.

Candide finally found his way back to Cunégonde, who was by now in Turkey. As he had always promised he would, he married her and bought a farm outside of Constantinople in hopes of living a simpler life. But, alas, the couple was unhappy. Sabine was disappointed as she read this part. A farm sounded just fine to her.

But she read on, and the end cheered her. When Candide met another farmer who taught him that tending to his own land could bring him true happiness, Candide began to sow the earth in earnest. He and Cunégonde grew so busy, and so committed to their land, that they no longer had time to think about what might make them happy. They had stopped trying so hard and searching so hard, and instead found peace and happiness by simply living their lives the way they wanted.

Sabine felt teary when she closed the book. She was envious of Candide's adventures. She suddenly understood Michel a little better—she understood everything a little better. What Candide and his friends did reminded her of what the colonists had done. They had sailed to the New World and built lives for themselves. And now the king of England wanted them to do things his way. *Well, no,* they were saying. *No, we're going to do this our own way. We're going to start over with a new government that is more fair than yours, and we're going to fight for this new government, this new country, because it matters and it is right.* They were willing to fight a war for what they had created. *How good that must feel,* she thought.

She thought of the marquis de Lafayette. Of course he wanted to go and join the battle. *People like us have nothing to fight for. Go,* she thought. *Go there and help them win. I would if I could.*

Sabine gave a start. Had she really just thought that? Would she really go across the ocean and leave her life in Paris behind? Oddly, she found her spirits lifting at the thought. For the first time in as long as she could remember, she fell asleep with a smile on her face.

Chapter Twelve

When morning came, Sabine didn't even bother with the dining room for breakfast. She bypassed her mother altogether and barged through the kitchen and out the kitchen door to the pantry. There, she found Cécile and Antoine, and their smiles reassured her that she belonged nowhere else.

"Morning, mademoiselle," Cécile offered as she curtsied.

"Cécile, please call me Sabine. And you too, Antoine." Sabine was positively giddy. She was starting fresh.

"All right, then." Cécile smiled. "How did it go with your mother?"

"Well"—Sabine thought for a minute—"it didn't go well," she said with a laugh. It was funny, actually. Margaux and her aspirations. The fact that she was willing to sell Sabine off to get what she wanted. What this meant to Sabine was that her mother did actually understand that Sabine was worth something, even though Margaux had always acted toward her as if she meant nothing and that she was a disappointment. Sabine realized that she felt liberated now. Maybe her mother didn't love her, but she *did* see value in her. And it was this fact that gave Sabine a confidence this morning that she had never once felt before.

She thought all this while Cécile and Antoine sat there, sipping coffee, waiting for her to finish her thought. Were they her friends now? It felt like it.

"Madem—er, Sabine," Antoine said, correcting himself, "since we're being honest, I must say I understand why you might not be inclined to marry Monsieur de Croy."

"I agree, Sabine," Cécile said, suddenly bubbling over. "I mean he's very handsome, dashing in fact"— she looked over at Antoine, who looked a little miffed at this—"but in a nasty way," she continued. "He's not at all charming or subtle and we all— rich or poor—want someone who *is,* mademoiselle." She blushed. It was as if Cécile just couldn't help calling Sabine "mademoiselle." Sabine smiled. This was how she had imagined Cécile all this time— cheerful and wise, without knowing that she was either.

They sat there for a while, talking about the tavern the night before and how Sabine had been so brazen and how the whole night was so unreal, and Sabine was beaming inside. This was what it was like to make friends on her own. The night at the tavern was the very first experience in her entire life that had been a result of her own doing.

They were laughing and chatting happily when Michel walked toward them. Sabine stiffened, but she was happy to see him. She wanted the opportunity to explain to him that she had had no knowledge of her engagement to Jean-Philippe, nor did she have any intention of honoring it. But Michel stormed by her.

"Cécile, Antoine," he grunted in their direction before reaching for the kitchen door.

Sabine grabbed his arm. She surprised herself when she did this and surprised Michel even more.

"I'm just here to check up on my mother, Sabine." He didn't even look at her when he said this.

"Michel," Sabine said firmly, "stop this. There will be no marriage for Jean-Philippe and me. I don't care who arranged what. I had nothing to do with it, and I've drawn the line. My mother and father might have made all kinds of decisions for me all my life, but not this one." She was talking loudly, and she felt good. She felt Cécile and Antoine's eyes on her as she spoke, and this only made her more comfortable. She felt as if they were on her side, and she was sure at this moment that she had never felt this way about anyone in her whole life.

"So, what shall we do about this, Sabine?" Michel said after a long pause. His body had relaxed, and he turned to her with a smile. *He is charming,* Sabine thought, *and subtle.*

"Well, what do you say we all move to a farm in Turkey?" she asked. She wanted Michel to know she had finished the book.

"I always liked that idea," Michel replied, clearly understanding her. "I was never very fond of Turkey, though." He looked at her. "How about a farm in America?"

Sabine smiled, and her eyes locked into Michel's. She could practically see herself in the darkness of his eyes, and she wanted to live in this pause for a while, rest for just a moment right here in Michel's stare, so she wouldn't have to think for a bit. And then she noticed that the little lines at the corners of his eyes, the ones that would become deep, laughing lines one day when he was older, hadn't crinkled one bit. Maybe he was serious. In this moment, Sabine and Michel's friendship deepened.

Before Sabine reluctantly excused herself, she asked Michel if he would stay at the house a bit longer, before returning to the Chaumont's, so they could meet again later that day. Then she dashed upstairs to ready herself for her family's encounter with the man she was set to marry. Jean-Philippe would be there shortly.

After some primping from a rather pale Brigitte, Sabine finally descended the staircase yet again, to find Jean-Philippe seated across from her mother. She noted that her father was not yet there and was not the least bit surprised. Why, this was only the engagement of his daughter. Surely he had more important matters to attend to.

Sabine managed to let Jean-Philippe greet her and kiss her hand without cringing, making sure her curtsy was as deep as she could manage. She wanted her face to be as far from his kiss as it could possibly be. She was about to be seated next to her suitor, when her father entered.

"Well, now, let's get on with this, de Croy," Georges Durand said without making eye contact with anyone. His eyes seemed to be glued to something just beyond them.

"Georges," Madame Durand protested in a sugary voice, "be kind, darling. This is just a formality, of course, but we want Jean-Philippe to know how pleased we are that he has chosen Sabine for his bride."

"But of course, madame," Jean-Philippe said now. "But I certainly understand the man's hurry. What father wouldn't be thrilled for this moment? To be rid of a daughter, and to see her off to a better place. Well, I can certainly understand the rush."

Georges Durand glared at Jean-Philippe. What was this? Sabine thought. Could her father be angry? Might he not support this engagement the way her mother did? Sabine waited in the awkward silence for him to defend his honor—to defend her. But the words never came.

"I'm sure Jean-Philippe simply means that we are thrilled to see our only daughter marry into one of the finest families in Paris," Madame Durand said, trying to ease the tension. Georges glanced in Sabine's direction, and she caught his eye. For just that second, Sabine thought that perhaps her father was on her side.

But then the moment had passed, and Georges Durand took the handshake offered by Jean-Philippe. The deal was done. They sat making small conversation until there was no more to say. And as soon as her parents were out of their seats and Jean-Philippe was out the door, Sabine practically ran to the pantry, where she found Michel waiting, just as he had said he would be. He smiled at her then, the kind of smile that fills the space between two people, and all was well in Sabine's world, if only for a moment.

• • •

Over the course of the next several weeks, Sabine and Michel's long-abandoned childhood friendship thrived once again, and they became closer than they had ever been, with Sabine plotting ways to get out of her engagement to Jean-Philippe and Michel making plans to sail to America. They were bonded now in their desperate pursuit of freedom.

With Cécile and Antoine's help, Sabine and Michel found each other by the pantry, on the kitchen steps, by the horses—all the places Madame Durand never, ever went. If her mother knew Sabine was spending any time at all with Michel, she would surely find a way to put an end to it. But Margaux was so consumed with her daughter's engagement that she had little time to be suspicious. And, aside from that, she knew that Brigitte hadn't been feeling well, so Michel's presence in her home was at least understandable.

It was only Élodie who seemed to know that something was very wrong. After letting the week after the opera pass without a word, she had begun sending notes to Sabine, apologizing for the misunderstanding. She wrote in her letters, *I do hope you'll come to see the romance of all this. We're going to be sisters,* chérie! But Sabine simply threw the notes in the trash.

Meanwhile, Sabine went along with her mother's extravagant wedding plans—nodding at Cook's menu ideas, smiling at the dressmaker's designs for her gown. She even entertained Jean-Philippe for tea once a week, letting him believe she was to be his. The wedding was to be in June, and she was told over and over that June brides are the most beautiful, and she smiled politely every time someone said this. She indulged all of this because she knew deep down inside her that the wedding simply wouldn't come to pass. She knew that as surely as the seasons would change, her life was going to change, too. And as winter melted into spring, the air brought with it the strong scent of hope.

Chapter Thirteen

Michel had taken to stopping by the side yard of the Durand household first thing, before his workday at the Chaumonts' began. He and Étienne were less close now since Dr. Chaumont had put more limits on their friendship. He had found out about the night at the tavern and wasn't pleased. He was a respectable man about town and expected that, if his son was going to go to taverns at all, he would go to one where young doctors and lawyers and businessmen drank their wine. Any other was a waste of time. This had pushed Michel even further to try to figure out where he fit in, and he and Sabine discussed this often.

Sabine sat outside one dewy April morning with Cécile—the two of them had grown quite close, not just because of their night out at the tavern, but because Brigitte needed more and more time to herself and Sabine turned to Cécile for little things like picking out dresses and gossiping about Jean-Philippe. In some ways, Cécile had taken the place of Élodie more than Brigitte had, which helped Sabine feel less guilty about confiding in her. She really missed spending time with Brigitte, and it felt strange that she couldn't share all the changes in her life. But Brigitte just wasn't up to it, and Sabine couldn't have told her anyway. The truth was, Brigitte would be upset that Sabine and Michel were spending time together. She was as fixed in her belief in the class system as Margaux was—she believed everyone had their place.

But Sabine wasn't thinking of any of this when she saw Michel come up the path. She was engrossed in conversation with Cécile, who was telling her about a talk she'd had with Antoine about marriage. Then, just as Michel came into sight, noises erupted in the kitchen, and Sabine felt right away that something was terribly wrong. Before she could even greet Michel, Cook burst out of the kitchen door. "Michel, come quick—your mother has collapsed!" he shouted.

Sabine and Michel didn't hesitate. Neither did Cécile. The three of them practically ran inside, only to find Brigitte slumped in a chair. "I did my best," Cook panted, "to get her up off the floor. This was the best I could do by myself."

"Someone get Dr. Chaumont!" Michel shouted. But Sabine was already out the door and running down the street toward his house. She ran so hard and fast that sweat was dripping down the sides of her face, despite the cool air. The Chaumont home wasn't far from hers by horse or carriage, but on foot it felt like miles. Finally, as she rounded the corner, the house came into sight and Sabine picked up speed as she ran toward the front door. She rapped so loudly her knuckles hurt. No one came. Then she slapped the door with the palms of both hands and shouted, "Please, we need help!" Finally, the door opened and Étienne stood before her.

"Sabine? What on earth?" Étienne asked, clearly concerned.

"Please, Étienne. Where is your father? Brigitte has fallen ill. She is unconscious." Étienne was gone then, having run off to find his father. Sabine stood there, anxiously tapping her foot. She started pacing and looking around to distract herself from the wait. She wandered into the library adjacent to the foyer, hoping they would hurry up. She saw books—so many books—and she calmed down for a moment. Her own parents didn't have many books, and the ones they did have looked untouched. These were leathery and worn. She ran her fingers across a shelf—Rousseau, Molière, Voltaire. Ha! She had a sudden rush of pride at having read this one.

Her insides jumping all around, Sabine wondered what was taking so long. She ran her nervous fingers across the bindings, tap-tap-tapping in the quiet room. She willed them to stop then and pulled a book from the shelf to distract herself from the anxiety in her belly. She couldn't bear to think that something might be really wrong with Brigitte. She shook off the idea and read the cover of the book. The title was *Le sens commun,* or *Common Sense,* by Thomas Paine. Sabine remembered that this was who Franklin had quoted—Thomas Paine was the American whose writing helped inspire the revolution! The book was positively dirty with overuse. Someone had flipped back and forth through the pages so many times, they seemed like they might fall from the binding. And so many pages were dog-eared. She flipped to one of them nervously. *We have it in our power to begin the world over again.* Someone had underlined that sentence, and Sabine understood why. Starting over sounded awfully good to her.

Soon she heard footsteps coming quickly. "Come, Sabine," Dr. Chaumont urged. He had his medical bag in his hand and was out of breath. She followed him to the carriage. In her haste, Sabine never put the book back, and on the bumpy ride to her house, she found herself clutching it, holding it tight to her chest, as if she were at church and it was her bible. *Please let Brigitte be all right,* she prayed.

Chapter Fourteen

Sabine, Michel, and Madame Durand hovered over the bed as Dr. Chaumont examined Brigitte. Sabine closed her eyes and willed the doctor to turn to them and say Brigitte would be fine, that she would be well soon, that she simply needed rest and lots of hot soup and tea.

But the doctor didn't say that. He couldn't. He looked at Michel with concern and put his hand on his arm.

"She has consumption, Michel," Dr. Chaumont said. "I don't know if she's going to make it."

Sabine turned to leave the room. She would make Brigitte tea anyway.

When Sabine returned from the kitchen, she found the Durand household quiet. It was night, and everyone had found their own space to sit and pray. Word of Dr. Chaumont's diagnosis had traveled through the house quickly, and the whole staff was holding a vigil outside her room, sitting on the floor, leaning against the wall. Sabine walked through the maze of them to get to Brigitte with the tea she had made especially—chamomile with mint leaves and honey. She opened the door slowly and saw that things hadn't improved since she had been gone. The flames of the candles flickered, casting eerie shadows on the ceiling, and Brigitte's breath was heavy and raspy, each inhale an effort.

Michel sat at the foot of the bed, reading from Brigitte's book of poetry. He hadn't left his mother's side since the moment he had found her slumped in her chair in the kitchen, and he was pale and worn as a result. Sabine couldn't believe how the beautiful eyes that had held her gaze so many times in recent weeks had turned so sad and drawn in a matter of hours.

"How are you, Brigitte?" Sabine whispered. "How is she?" she asked Michel when she realized Brigitte was in no shape to answer her.

"Her breathing seems worse to me," Michel said without looking at Sabine. "Mother," he said to Brigitte, who turned to him now. Michel's voice was shaky, and Sabine found this hard to hear. He had always been tough and coolheaded, even as a child. Sabine had never seen him show much emotion. Now, Sabine realized, *she* must be the strong one. She put her hand on Michel's shoulder, and Brigitte looked at them for a minute and opened her mouth to speak.

"That's nice," she said quietly. "You'll take care of each other now."

"No, Brigitte, we won't have to," Sabine said cheerfully. "We won't have to because we'll always have you to take care of us." She sat down close to

Brigitte now and helped her sip some tea. "You see, that's good. You'll be better in no time, and you'll help me figure out what to do about Jean-Philippe and Mother and Élodie, and we'll make sense of all the nonsense. Right, Brigitte? You'll be better in no time." Sabine squeezed Brigitte's hand as she swallowed her tears.

"Yes, Sabine." Brigitte said what Sabine wanted to hear.

Madame Durand came in then, and after checking Brigitte's head and changing the washcloths for fresh ones—she was all business, of course—she ordered Sabine to let Brigitte get some rest.

But when Sabine got up to go, Michel took her hand, and she stopped. Michel's touch sent her a powerful message—he wanted her to stay. Sabine's heart pounded, and she knew she had to admit to herself why. She had fallen in love with Michel, and she would not—could not—leave him.

Aware that her mother was watching, her impulse

was to let his hand go and proceed to her room. Instead, she squeezed it tight, turned around, and stood by him.

"I think I'll stay here, Mother," Sabine said.

Madame Durand sucked her teeth hard and turned to leave, but not before having the last word: "Michel, I understand that your mother is dying, and I am sorry for it. She has been a faithful servant. But you will still mind your place in this house-hold." Her voice revealed no emotion. It was steady and cold. "She will be missed. Both of you will be missed."

Sabine turned to her mother then. "What is that supposed to mean?"

"Sabine, Brigitte will be gone soon, and so will Michel. Dr. Chaumont and I both believe it's time for Michel to move on."

Then she walked out the door without a noise.

Sabine was seething. First, she could not believe her mother would say that Brigitte was dying! Dr. Chaumont had said there was a chance she could survive—they had all heard him say that. Never mind the fact that she had said it right in front of Brigitte. And then to tell Michel that Dr. Chaumont was letting him go and that she had been in on that decision! Her mother had outdone herself, and Sabine wouldn't have it. She followed her mother into the hallway.

"What are you doing?" She was whispering and shouting at her mother at the same time.

"What am *I* doing?" Margaux had turned around and was staring at Sabine with fiery eyes. "I think the better question is, What are *you* doing, Sabine? I am taking care of my family. I am making sure you have a respectable future as part of a respectable family. I am doing all this for you while you are holding hands with the help. Well, no more. When Brigitte is gone—and Sabine, she *is* dying—Michel will be gone, too, and things will go back to normal around here. I tried to get rid of that boy years ago, but moving him down the street wasn't good enough, was it? I was too nice about the whole thing, and I'm paying for it now. So get used to the idea of life without Michel."

"I will do no such thing." Sabine couldn't believe she said that, but she went on. "You can kick Michel out of this house, and Dr. Chaumont can fire him, but what do you think? That he will be gone and suddenly I'll fall in love with Jean-Philippe instead?" She choked a little on the lump creeping up her throat. She knew Brigitte was dying, and it was all she could do to keep herself from shaking with grief.

"What do you mean 'instead'? You can't mean that you're in love with Michel. Oh, Sabine!" Her mother laughed at her.

Sabine hadn't realized what she had said, but she was smart enough to know that she should deny her words.

"Of course I am not in love with Michel, Mother. But I am certainly not and never will be in love with Jean-Philippe."

"You don't need to be in love, darling. I honestly don't know where you came from. Marriage is an arrangement, Sabine, and we have made a wonderful one for you. Love isn't for the likes of us; it's for the peasants, who have nothing to lose."

Her mother walked away from her without another word, and Sabine understood something now. Her parents didn't love each other at all. Her mother didn't know love. No one who had known true love could ever bear to live without it.

Sabine went back into Brigitte's room and quietly pulled a chair to the side of the bed. She took Brigitte's hand and listened as Michel read to his mother through the night.

Sabine knew love.

Chapter Fifteen

Sabine woke up where she had fallen asleep—in the chair next to Brigitte's bed. Michel was standing by the window. "She's gone," he said as he stared outdoors. Sabine looked at Brigitte. She was still. The room was still and as quiet as anything Sabine had ever experienced.

"No," Sabine said in a low voice. She put her hand on Brigitte's chest, hoping for a heartbeat. There was none. "But Dr. Chaumont said—"

Michel cut her off. "Dr. Chaumont was being kind. She had no chance." Michel still hadn't looked at her. He was talking to the tree outside the window.

Sabine felt ill. She sucked back a sob. She wasn't ready to cry yet. If she did, the tears might never stop. Brigitte was gone, and so was the only mother Sabine had ever really known. Sabine was suddenly overwhelmed; she never wanted to leave this room, because once she did, she would be truly alone. In here, with Brigitte and Michel, she felt like part of a family.

"Michel, what are we going to do without her?" Sabine asked. "I honestly don't know what to do now. I can't even get out of this chair. I cannot leave this room and go back to my life. To my mother and Élodie and all the nonsense. I can't." Sabine started to cry.

"Then don't." Michel finally turned to look at her, and she looked up at him.

"What?" she asked. "How?"

"Sabine, I've been planning to leave here for a long time. I only stayed here for my mother. I have plans. I'm going to find a way to go to America."

Sabine was shocked. *America!* They had just

dreamed of going there, of course. They talked about it all the time. But for her it was a dream, something she would pretend she might actually do—but never really do. How could Michel go to America? How could he leave Paris and everything he knew to go to a place he'd never laid eyes on? Sabine knew he wanted to go and she understood why. But she felt things had changed. How could he leave her?

"But they're at war, Michel." This was all she could think to say.

"I know. And I want to fight with them."

Sabine felt devastation setting in. Brigitte was gone, and now Michel was going to leave just when he had come back into her life, just when her whole life was changing.

"Why did you bother with me, then?" Sabine demanded. "Why get me thinking about revolution and change? About . . . you?" She said the last part with hesitation, knowing that she was admitting for the first time out loud her feelings for him. But she went on: "Why do all that if you were just going to leave me here? Why would you do that?"

Michel walked toward her and knelt at her lap.

"I wouldn't. I'm not," he whispered, and Sabine looked at him, puzzled. "You're going to come with me."

Sabine's heart skipped, but she said, "To America? I can't go to America. That's just ridiculous." Michel looked hurt, but she knew she was right. It *was* ridiculous. "I mean, how would we get there? Where would we live? How could I leave?"

"How could you leave what? Your mother? Jean-Philippe? If you stay, she will find a way to make you marry him, and you will spend the rest of your life going to balls and the opera and having tea with Élodie, chattering mindlessly about a world that is fading. Sabine, believe me, people are talking revolution here, too. One day, there will be no king, no aristocracy. It will be a big fight, to be sure, but things will change here just like in America."

"But if you hate the entire aristocracy, then you hate me, too," Sabine countered. "That's who I am, Michel. I just don't know if I could leave here with nothing and start a new life in a new world. I don't know if I belong there. I'm not sure where I belong anymore." Sabine was suddenly sobbing. Brigitte was dead, Michel was leaving, and there they were discussing a future in a new world. Soon, the room would be flooded with people, and Sabine might never get to finish this conversation. She had to think fast, but she had never been so confused.

"I don't know either," Michel said at last. "But I know that I don't belong here. And sometimes, knowing where you don't belong can be even more telling than knowing where you do. And you've never belonged here, either, Sabine. Even when we were little and you tried to act as if you were better than me, as if you were a princess and I was a servant. Well, that wasn't you. I knew it wasn't, but you had to do what was expected of you—behave like a well-brought-up young lady who took tea with girl-friends and planned to marry a *duc,* or in your case, the son of a *duc,* eh? Well, you tried that, didn't you? And it wasn't you. Come with me now. Let's find out where we belong." Michel was practically begging her. "This is your chance to do something, to affect the way things turn out—"

Just then, the doors burst open and Madame Durand barged in with Dr. Chaumont. "How long has she been like this?" she asked accusingly. The doctor rushed to Brigitte's side and calmly checked her neck, then nodded in Madame Durand's direction.

Michel quickly whispered to Sabine that she should meet him by the pantry later, then he muttered something to Dr. Chaumont, asking the doctor to make the arrangements for Brigitte. At that, Sabine couldn't hold the tears back for one more second. She let out a wail that hurt as it came up from her chest, and she collapsed onto the floor. She sat there with her wet face in her hands for what seemed like hours. Michel came over to her; Dr. Chaumont came over to her, Cécile rushed in and came over to her. But her mother did not come. Madame Durand stood still for a moment and then walked out of the room, passing by her sobbing heap of a daughter as if she weren't there at all.

Chapter Sixteen

No sooner had the coroner taken Brigitte's body away than Michel was out the door. Sabine couldn't help feeling that he was running away from his mother's death. And she didn't blame him. Life without Brigitte would be bleak, and she had to consider whether she wanted to go on with her charade of a life. For the first time ever, she felt she had a choice. Michel had given her that gift.

On her way to meet Michel by the pantry, Sabine had to stop to see her mother in the drawing room. Sabine was perturbed at having to talk to her on the way to do something important. Besides, she didn't know if her mission would show on her face, and she didn't want her mother to suspect anything.

"Sabine, we're going to the de Croy home for supper. Be sure to wear something special. At last, we're going to meet the esteemed Mr. Franklin."

If only she knew that he and I are old friends already, Sabine thought.

"Mother, Brigitte died today. You can't possibly think it appropriate to go there now," Sabine replied coolly.

"It is quite sad, I admit. But she wasn't family, and I should think it would be difficult to explain to the *duchesse* de Croy that we are canceling because someone on our staff passed away. Don't you think it would be inappropriate? I mean, not only will the Fourniers be there, celebrating Élodie's engagement and yours, but so will Mr. Benjamin Franklin. We just cannot cancel now." Madame Durand was genuinely nervous, and Sabine found it pathetic.

"By the way, dear, I would ask for your help in replacing her, but you were getting a bit old for a governess, and I think perhaps a maidservant will be enough now," Margaux added.

This was true, Sabine thought. She didn't really need a governess anymore, but a mother would have been nice.

Sabine assured her mother that she'd be there just so she could end the conversation. Finally, she made it to the pantry, and she discovered Michel inside, loading up a burlap sack with food.

"What are you doing?" Sabine asked.

"I'm leaving for Bordeaux tonight, and I need some food for my journey," he replied. Sabine noted that he was taking food from her pantry and not from the Chaumonts'. He was mad at her family.

"Bordeaux? Why? What journey?" Sabine knew her tone revealed how anxious she was. "You're leaving for America *now*?"

"Well, you were right before, Sabine. When I was hard on the aristocracy, I suppose I was hasty. I should have known that if there was one good aristocrat, there would be more." He winked at her when he said this, but she was confused. "Anyway, one of your peers seems to have gotten a ship together and is heading to America. He's going to be a major general in the American service, and I'm going with him. We're going to help them win their independence, Sabine."

"The marquis de Lafayette," Sabine said. She knew instantly that was who Michel meant.

"Yes. You knew?"

"I had heard he wanted to go, and I had hoped he'd find a way. I didn't know when I hoped that for him that he would be taking you with him." Sabine was feeling mad and manipulated. "So that's it?" she added. "After your speech this morning, daring me to go with you to America, you decide you're better off without me?"

"No! This is just my way there. We couldn't have gone together—we would have been stopped for sure," Michel explained. "I have a way for you, too, but you must wait until I find out where I'll be in

America before we get you on a ship. What do you say?" He was so excited, he didn't seem to be making any sense at all.

"What do I say to what?" What was he asking her—if she would travel to America by herself to meet him?

"Étienne is coming with me, too. We're traveling together to Bordeaux. There is some resistance to what the marquis is doing. The king all but forbade him to leave, and even Mr. Franklin, who had been encouraging him to go, has backed down. So we are leaving in secret. Tonight, before we depart for Bordeaux, we will find out where we will be settling in America. Meet me at the Chaumonts', Sabine, and we'll make sure you get on the next ship to America."

"Does Dr. Chaumont know?" Sabine asked. She couldn't imagine he did, after what her mother had told her earlier.

"Yes," Michel said. "I know your mother told you that he was going to fire me, but that was part of his plan. He couldn't let on to people that he was in favor of Étienne and me going to America. I was coming over here yesterday to tell you."

Sabine was floored. This was happening so fast. "I can't tonight," she said. "My parents are expecting me at a dinner at the de Croys. Apparently Mr. Franklin will be there." She was preoccupied for a moment, wondering how she would explain it to her mother if Mr. Franklin should recognize her. She reassured herself that there was no way a man like him would remember a girl like her. "Anyway, I cannot get out of it." She was actually thinking that she probably could, but for some reason, she wanted the excuse not to go and meet Michel. It was too much for her.

"Sabine, please try. It's the only way," Michel urged.

"If I don't . . . if I *can't*, will I never see you again?" Sabine asked.

"If you want to see me again, you will be there." Michel was looking at her with an intensity that stripped her of her veneer. With Michel, she never could be polite and vague. He demanded honesty from her and forced her to be who she really was. It was frightening and exhilarating at once.

If this was good-bye, she had to do something. She walked over to him and put her hand on his face.

"If I don't come, it isn't because I don't love you. I think I do love you." Sabine paused, half hoping he would return the sentiment. When he didn't, she continued. "But I don't know if I can do this, so please just say good-bye to me now just in case."

"I won't say good-bye, because it isn't good-bye," Michel said as he brushed her hand away. "I know you'll be there. Now," he said as he squeezed her hands in his, "I have to go. I'll see you later. And once we both get to America, I'll see you forever." Michel let go of her hands and ran off toward the street. Soon, he disappeared from her sight, and Sabine thought, *I'll see you in my dreams.*

Chapter Seventeen

Getting dressed for dinner at the de Croys' was tricky for Sabine. She kept expecting Brigitte to walk through the door and, in her businesslike way, go about laying out Sabine's dress, pinning her hair, pulling her corset. She was sure she had decided not to meet Michel tonight, but she couldn't let herself think she might never see him again, so she pretended to herself that she might still go.

She chose a black dress—the same dress she had worn to her grandmother's funeral last year. She wanted to honor the memory of Brigitte. The black dress hung right next to the dress she wore the day she sat for Fragonard, and she wondered if she'd ever see that painting. She hoped for an instant that she would, years from now, come across it and smile knowing that she was, after all, as interesting a subject as the ones she had imagined as a young girl.

When Sabine and her parents arrived, everyone was in fine spirits. The de Croys' home was stunning, and the supper table was decked out as if for the king himself—candles and crystal, china and flowers. It looked nothing like Madame Chaumont's table and reminded Sabine of the ball her mother had thrown. It felt to her as if years had passed since that night, and it had only been four short months.

When she saw Jean-Philippe, Sabine felt a knot form in her stomach. Then she greeted Élodie, who gave her hugs and kisses as if nothing had ever happened between them to change things.

"I'm so sorry about Brigitte, darling. I know how much you adored her. But cheer up. This is a lovely party, isn't it?" Sabine was annoyed at her friend's airs. This was all so fake. The knot in her stomach tightened. She knew now why she was so much more comfortable with Michel and Cécile and Antoine than she was with the people in this room. It was because, as her mother herself had said, people like Michel didn't have much to lose. But Sabine's parents and their friends, and Élodie too—they were fiercely protecting something that was invisible to her. Their money, maybe, but something else, too. Their status, their place in Parisian society. Sabine realized now that if they lost that, they would have nothing. *How sad for all of them,* she thought.

Just then, Madame Durand interrupted Sabine's thoughts. She was clicking her glass with a knife from the table, in order to call the room to attention.

She cleared her throat and said in her haughtiest voice, "It is an honor to be with all of you tonight to celebrate this joyous and momentous occasion—three grand families joining together as one. The Fourniers, the de Croys, and the Durands!" She paused as the room erupted with clinks of toasting glasses. Sabine stood still. Her mother continued: "We couldn't let this night pass without a gesture on our part, so Georges and I present to you"—as she spoke, Sabine realized that her mother was standing beside an easel, and suddenly she understood what was about to happen—"Monsieur Fragonard's portrait of Sabine Durand!"

With a grand gesture, Madame Durand flung the cloth off of the easel. Sabine continued to stand still even as the crowd around her celebrated with applause and rave reviews. *"C'est magnifique!"* "One of his best, to be sure!" "Jean-Philippe is a lucky man, indeed!"

Sabine walked toward the painting and stared at herself. It was beautiful. There was an exquisite glow emanating from the canvas, and Sabine realized that Fragonard had been right—the light mattered a great deal. He had really captured her—the intensity with which she was reading, her restless fingers at peace holding her book. These things were visible to everyone in the room, but only Sabine could see the rumblings of dissatisfaction in the girl in the painting. Only Sabine could see that there was sadness deep inside that girl, and dreams of bigger things, better places, wild adventures. *How sad for them, but not for me,* she said to herself, finishing the thought her mother had interrupted.

In that moment, Sabine determined that she wouldn't let their lives be *her* life. She would make choices for herself, starting tonight. Sitting for that painting had been the beginning of something special, and seeing it finished would mark another beginning for Sabine. The painting was beautiful, she realized, because it captured the moment she had stopped being one of them.

A weight lifted suddenly, and it became easy for Sabine to stand with Jean-Philippe and endure the endless chatter around her. She decided to give in and became animated and at ease in the group for the first time in her life. She even managed to blush as her mother sang Jean-Philippe's praises.

"Oh, yes, Mother," Sabine agreed, "he certainly is handsome. I am a lucky girl." Madame Durand seemed delighted at her daughter's mood, nodding in the direction of Georges Durand, and he nodding back, as if he even cared. Strangely, her mother didn't seem the least bit suspicious of Sabine's turn-around. It was like her not to question such a thing, not to question anything at all. This blindness, this willful blindness, was the very thing that irked Sabine so much about her mother. Where Sabine wanted knowledge and progress, her mother wanted none. Sabine realized now that this was the rift she had been trying to repair her whole life, but it was clear tonight that it was beyond repair. There was nothing more she could do; there probably never had been.

Just then, Mr. Franklin's arrival was announced, and Sabine took it as a final sign solidifying her decision. Seeing him reminded her of the night at the Chaumonts', of the way she had felt when she walked out into the early morning air with Michel.

Suddenly she was absolutely sure of what she was doing. She walked toward the American.

"Good evening, Mademoiselle Sabine," Benjamin Franklin said, and kissed her hand. He remembered her!

"Good evening, sir. It is lovely to see you again." Sabine felt the room quiet down behind her, and she turned to see her mother looking perplexed. She was delighted that she got to see the expression on Margaux's face. Her simple burden of a daughter had met this great man before her, and she had even been memorable. What a wonderful way to take her last look at her mother. "Please forgive me," she said to Mr. Franklin, "but I have somewhere I have to go."

"Somewhere good, I hope," Mr. Franklin said with a smile.

"Yes, sir, I think you would approve." Sabine curtsied and looked at her mother again, who was trying desperately to hide her confusion. "Mother, please understand that I have to go now," Sabine said. And then she looked at the group—Élodie, Jean-Philippe, her father—all of whom looked as though they were struggling to figure out what was going on. Sabine was sad and hurt, and yet she would miss them all. She waited for the tears welling behind her eyes to dry up before she continued. "I hope you all have a wonderful evening."

Then she ran out the door, but she heard her mother behind her.

"Sabine! Where do you think you're going?" Margaux was following her. Sabine was nervous that her mother would catch up to her and that she would somehow convince her or threaten her into staying, but that didn't happen at all.

"Margaux!" It was Georges Durand's voice, and it stopped both Margaux and Sabine in their tracks. "Go inside," he said to his wife. Margaux smirked at him. "Now," he said strongly. Margaux looked at Sabine and then headed back inside. This was the only time in her entire life Sabine could remember hearing her father's voice rising above a whisper. "Sabine," he said, his voice softening again. Sabine felt compelled to listen to him.

"You have a great-aunt in Rheims. It isn't as far away as America, but I think it's far enough from here that you'll be able to find something you've been searching for your whole life. Your aunt Geneviève was my mother's sister, and she found a way out of all this. I think you've needed her for a long time now. No one will know where you are— I promise."

Sabine was stunned. She had planned to meet Michel at the Chaumonts', even though she suspected that he was already gone. She hadn't actually thought of where she would go from there. She only knew that she wasn't going home.

"How will she know to expect me?" she asked, feeling like a little girl and wishing she were, wishing her father would take her up into his lap and protect her. Sabine realized that he was trying to do this now.

"I wrote to her after your engagement. I told her you might be coming for a visit."

Sabine looked at him. "But why—how—?"

"You and I are more alike than you know, Sabine. I never wanted this either, but I have never been strong enough or brave enough to let go of it entirely. You are strong enough, and this is the only way I can think of to help you. This is your best way out. Now, go," he said. "I'll take care of your mother." He handed her a slip of paper with an address and directions.

"Thank you," she said, and turned toward the carriage. She got a few steps away and turned back again, walking briskly toward her father. She went to wrap her arms around him but was stopped short. He couldn't pull her in. Instead, he gripped her forearms tight, keeping her from getting too close to him. He loosened his grip with one hand and cupped her chin with it. Sabine understood that this was all her father was capable of, but she was grateful. She was relieved that he cared enough to risk so much for her and relieved that she had so much in common with him. It made her feel as if she did have a family, after all.

"You are going to be just fine, darling, and so will I. Now, go on," he said, and went back into the party.

And as she hopped into the carriage, Antoine got the horses moving quickly. "Where are we going, mademois—er, Sabine?" he yelled back to her.

"Here," she said, handing him the paper, "but we have a stop or two to make first."

It was a warm night, the kind of night that tricks you into thinking spring has really arrived, but then you wake up the next day to the coldest air you've ever felt all winter long. Sabine breathed deeply as the indigo dusk fell on Paris. *Please be there, Michel,* she prayed. *Please, please, please.* She wouldn't go with him—of that she was now certain. But she wanted to talk to him one last time, to tell him what he meant to her. When the carriage arrived, she hopped out just as the horses slowed, but landed steady on the moist ground.

Just the day before, she had rushed to this same front door, hoping to save Brigitte. When Sabine banged on the door this time, Dr. Chaumont answered right away, and from the look on his face, Sabine could tell she was too late.

"He left you a note," he said as he showed her into the library. Sabine's hands were shaking as she took the note from the doctor and uncurled it.

Dear Sabine,

I waited as long as I could. Did you really decide to stay? I suppose that if you did, you are not reading this letter at all and it has instead made its way to the trash bin. And in that case, I am heartbroken that I will not see you again and that you have made the wrong choice. But that is the downside of free will, eh? People may not make the right decisions.

Oh, but if you are reading this, then you came! Will you meet me in a place called Philadelphia? Ask Dr. Chaumont—he'll help you. I have to go now. Come to America, Sabine . . . and we'll start the world over again.

Love, Michel

Philadelphia, thought Sabine. *What a lovely name for a city.* She didn't know what it meant. She didn't know one word of English, but to her, Philadelphia sounded like a fine place to start the world all over again.

Michel's last phrase reminded her of something. Sabine looked up at Dr. Chaumont with tears in her eyes. "I stole your book," she said. "I stole *Common Sense* yesterday morning when I came for you. I was waiting in the library and I came across it, and in our haste to leave, I just took it." She was rambling, and Dr. Chaumont touched her arm to quiet her.

"Keep it," he told her. "If you're going to be a revolutionary, you'll need it."

Sabine said her good-byes to the Chaumonts and headed back to the carriage.

Antoine took Sabine home so she could gather some things for her journey. Cécile met her outside when the carriage arrived.

"How did you know I'd be back so soon?" Sabine asked Cécile.

"I didn't, but I hoped." Cécile smiled, and Sabine grabbed her hand as they ran inside.

Sabine knew Cécile thought they were packing for a trip to America. "He's gone already, Cécile," Sabine told her friend, and with that, tears burned her eyes. She suddenly felt the pain of Michel's being gone. Cécile hugged her tight and said nothing until Sabine stopped crying. When they finally pulled apart, Cécile spoke.

"So, what then? Where are you going?" she asked.

"Well, apparently I have an aunt who is expecting me. Can you imagine? I'm really going to be rid of Mother. This is really happening!"

Cécile looked sad. "I'm so happy for you," she said, now a little teary herself.

Sabine stopped for a moment. "Cécile, we'll see each other again. I know we will."

"We'll have a whole night's journey to talk about that. I'm coming with you—Rheims is too far to go alone."

Sabine was thrilled to have Cecile for a traveling companion. Sabine changed quickly into the least assuming dress she owned. It was burgundy and simple and put her in the mind of Mr. Franklin's simple brown suit. Sabine hoped it would do. She packed a small bag, threw in her copies of *Candide* and *Common Sense,* and was off.

Sabine sat dreamily next to Cécile in the carriage. She had not looked back at her house. Brigitte had died there, and part of Sabine had died there, too. As they headed out into the country, Sabine had the butterflies most people get when they're on their way to something wonderful—the opera for some, a picnic in the country for others. For her it was this—heading in the direction of something entirely different, never to return.

It was a quiet journey. The girls slept most of the night away as Antoine kept steadily on the horses.

In the very early hours of the morning, just before the sun was to come up, they arrived at her aunt's house.

Sabine stirred as the carriage shook and bounced over the rough terrain approaching the house. It was dark outside, but Sabine could see that it was a small house with a long path and, from the scent in the air, that it was surrounded by overgrown lavender and verbena. It smelled like summer. When the carriage finally came to a stop, they all stepped out onto the damp, cold ground. There wasn't much left to say. This was good-bye for now and they all knew it. Sabine kissed Cécile good-bye and thanked her for her friendship one last time.

"Good-bye, mademoiselle." Cécile smiled through her tears.

Sabine nodded at Antoine then, and he nodded back, hopping up onto his perch. As she headed up the path, Sabine thought back to the night of the ball. She understood now that the freedom she had been seeking that night was here. She had escaped, disappeared—not into her duvet but into the cool Paris night.

Just then, a light turned on, and Sabine picked up her pace. The night wasn't so dark anymore. Sabine didn't know if she would ever find her way to America, and she realized that was all right with her. When she had hesitated earlier, when Michel asked her to go with him, Sabine was afraid that if she said yes, she'd have been going for him. Now, because he had left without her, because she had no idea if she'd ever lay eyes on him again, she knew why she was leaving Paris for somewhere else. She was hoping to find something that was suddenly the most important thing in the world to her. She was hoping to find herself.

ACKNOWLEDGMENTS

This book is dedicated to my husband, Jon, who is not only the best friend I will ever have, but a dear friend to history as well. Benjamin Franklin came to life on these pages because of him.

I want to also thank my children, Grace Eden and Elijah Henry, whose tiny faces and giant, intelligent eyes inspire me every day of my life. Thank you to my mother, Gail Seidel Levine, whose support of me as a writer and a mother is unparalleled, and who is a better editor than she knows.

I could not have written this book without the support of my dad, Charles Levine; my brother, Michael Levine (if only Sabine had a big brother like you); my wonderful mother- and father-in-law, Meryl and Stewart Ain; my grandmother-in-law, Helen Fischman, whose compelling stories reminded me to take notes all the time—she is greatly missed; my dear friend Chava Ortner for being there during all three of my labors (this book being the third); and our babysitter and surrogate little sister, Darcy Kaplan.

I also want to say that I would not have sent this book out to one publisher if it were not for Amy (Griffin) Betz, whose hiring of me back in the day was my first big break, and whose exceptional friendship has brought with it tremendous opportunities and support.

In the course of writing this book, I lost my grandmother Reba Seidel. It is beyond sad to me that she will never read it. She was the greatest supporter my writing has known, and she is missed every single day.

Last but not least, thank you to my editor, Hilary Van Dusen, for believing in this book, and challenging me to make it so much better.

Thank you all so much.